# Evil in the Heavenly Realms

## by Teisha Christie

I0637903

Evil in the Heavenly Realms

## Dedication

This book is dedicated to Carol Brown. Ma, I finished the book! My mother would always ask me: "When are you gonna finish that book? That must be some book you're writing!" The question motivated and inspired me every time she asked. When tremendous obstacles presented themselves, I would hear my mother's voice and keep on going.  At the age of sixty-five, my mother picked up a paintbrush to paint and pursue her dream of becoming an artist. Also, this book is dedicated to all the beautiful Black women that died with a dream in their hearts because they were burdened with responsibilities. Creativity is a luxury that many cannot afford.  This book is for those who had stories in their minds but did not have pen, ink, or paper.  To those who painted on canvases that they could not afford and had to choose alternative mediums. Thank you for paving the way to enable me to create.  Finally, this book is for my little sisters. Wherever you are, I see you, I hear you, and I love you.

Thank you heavenly father for empowering me and confirming that I have the right to write what I want. I am the prayer of those who came before me.  There was tremendous spiritual traffic that delayed this book from getting to you.  The story of soul ties has been in my spirit for over ten years. The characters danced in my head in the middle of the night. They would not go away even when it seemed I would never finish.  They each started with bones and over time gained muscle, flesh, personalities, and eventually became full grown characters.  I am grateful to my friends that listened to my disjointed thoughts and ideas and encouraged me to keep going and showed great interest in the story that did not have a beginning, middle, or end.  Writing is my purpose and one of the reasons God put me on earth. When I am writing I am executing true love.  If you are reading this book you are making my dream come true and I am grateful. Thank you from the best of my heart.

## Ephesians 6:11

Put on the whole armor of God, so that you can take your stand against the devil's schemes. For our struggle is not against flesh and blood, but against the rulers, against the authorities, against the powers of this dark world and against the spiritual forces of evil in the heavenly realms.

## 1

## OPEN

Last week, Sky made the critical mistake of purposely missing his call.  She imagined his smell and taste of him all week which led to her fever.  The kind of fever that was figurative but made the body hot with lust rising from the feet, caressing the legs, up the thighs, making her warm core pulse, crawling up the spine around to the breast and neck and up through the head. The kind of fever that needed to be addressed or it would follow a person down the street, into meetings, and everywhere he or she went.

She felt her body betraying her daily and could not take it anymore. She called him, and as usual, he was on the way. Sky selected layers of clothing for their pleasure and excited herself as her fingertips moved back and forth over the fishnets, lace, red thong, and silky fabric of her lingerie prior to his arrival.

She grew anxious and between her legs pumped fiercely as she waited for the alert from her video image system. "Bloopt, Bloopt" the motion sensor alerted her announcing he was downstairs.  Sky looked at her camera system and the rhythms of her heart moved faster when his image flashed on the screen. She saw Marlon in his blue and white pin striped suit with his sunglasses on. He turned toward her direction to acknowledge her presence, followed by his smile. "Hey Skit!" Marlon's deep voice caressed her.  Sky felt streams of wetness soak through her panties and her kegel muscle contracting at the sound of his voice.  She watched him unlock the door with his code and entered. Sky's condo was built inside of a ship that was converted to be open and modern. It was almost two football fields long and the height rivaled many of the other buildings on the Boston Skyline. The middle of the ship was hollow, and Marlon looked up and could not see her house from the ground floor. The long white massive hallway made it seem like an eternity for Marlon to get upstairs.

Marlon was so excited his heart raced, and he could feel small sweat beads forming above his lip and on his forehead. The elevator rising was synonymous with the rising temperature of his body. He could feel the temperature rise in his hands and ears as he got closer to her floor. He floated down the hallway to her door.

He put his key in the lock and entered the apartment, but she was nowhere in sight. He smiled to himself and began to look around for her. Sky watched him walk in the apartment gracefully, cool, and smooth. His crisp white shirt perfectly complemented the pin striped stitches in his suit. The shirt begins to stick to his chest.  His movement of walking past her and the trail of his smell aroused Sky. She walked behind him and stuck the cold gun barrel in his back. Marlon smiled with anticipation of this game and said, "Please, you don't have to do this."

As they walked further into the apartment, she instructed, "Shut up and sit down." Marlon sat on the table in the middle of the room and did not object. Sky put the gun on the table where he could see it but could not reach it and then turned up the volume on the music and slowly rubbed her body with her own hands.  She began twisting her waist and torso in a circular slithering motion. Sky was desperate to see Marlon's eyes on her and when she turned around, he was completely captivated. Sky started removing her first layer with twists and shoulder rolls. She slowly tugged the belt on her robe to reveal her see through leopard print lingerie and seductively glided the robe down her hips. He leaned back and watched her with hooded eyes. She bent over to remove the robe and he saw her red G-string through her fishnet body stocking.

Marlon silently mouthed the words, "You nasty motherfucker." She hypnotically grinded her body towards him and rubbed her body against the bulge in the front of his pants. His hands were still a little cold from being outside, but he attempted to touch her. She slapped his hand, "Don't touch!" she said. She picked the gun up again to remind him he was still in danger and then she kissed him. The kiss she gave him was so sweet and executed to perfection that it added to his already horny state. He watched her dark huge areolas and hard nipples sit on top of her full breasts bursting through the fishnets. His eyes traveled down her tight small stomach and stopped on her wide hips.

She turned around and her full round juicy bottom was completely consumed by the red thong. She handed him two shots of his favorite cognac and then waved him on. She said, "Follow me" and began leading him into the kitchen. Marlon was pleased to oblige. As he followed Sky to the kitchen table, her round ass cheeks jiggled. He watched her climb the chair and sat on her tall kitchen table and seductively spread her legs as he took his seat. She gently tugged the belt from around her waist and slithered it off slowly and seductively placed it around his neck with a smile and said, "Eat it." She licked the gun to remind him he was in danger. The red panties trapped between her wet lips looked beautiful to him with her legs spread wide. He spread the lips between her legs gently with his fingers and was greeted by clear slippery bubbles and she smelled like olive oil. A distinct smell that he could never forget. Sky watched Marlon's head between her legs deliver the perfect amount of suction, pressure, speed, and gentleness.

This is what she had been waiting for all week. She felt him move his tongue in little circles that turned into big circles as he increased his speed. He told her, "Take your time baby, give it to me." Marlon replaced his tongue with his hand and moved in fast circles and went back with his tongue. He said, "Leave it all in my mouth." Sky helped him take off his shirt revealing what looked like a platter of chocolate consisting of a thick neck, wide chest, rock hard abs, and broad shoulders covered.

He flipped her around moving from between her legs to her juicy bottom and slowly sucked. He moved his hands fast between her legs in the front while he enjoyed tasting her from the back. Sky felt delicious, dangerous, and alive. She heard his lips slurping her nether lips and the warmth of his tongue inside of her hot box from behind and the speed of his fingers on her clitoris. He flipped her back around with ease with what seemed like a simple flex of his muscles. He continued between her legs and she watched the muscles in his shoulders and back contract with the rhythm of his suction. He heard her breathing slowing down and knew she was preparing to cum when she held her breath and clutched his head as her clitoris grew large and pulsed. The only sound Marlon heard was his own slurping while he felt the belt tightening around his neck. As she began to shake and her body pulsed, she pulled his head closer into her body and he freely stuck his tongue deeper into her. He filled his palms with her bottom squeezing and inhaling. His head buried in her core wetting his face as though he were eating a scrumptious meal. Her body began to quiver beneath him. He knew she was done when she was able to speak again.

"Marlon?" Sky said.

"I'm here," He responded.

He moved his head towards hers and she received his lips.

"You're so good," she yelled loudly and freely, shaking her head furiously back and forth.

She slowly climbed off the table slid down on her knees and looked up into his eyes and he looked at her with passion and weakness like she was the only woman left on earth. She slowly finished unbuckling his pants and removed the belt from his neck and placed the belt around her own neck. She tightened it and handed him the gun and the strap to the belt. She removed his pants in one motion, took off his underwear, and ran her tongue from the top of his stomach down to the hairline of his pubis and kept going down to the crease on the left side of his balls and then the right side, and to the bottom of the balls between his legs. "You're so hard," Sky said.

His manhood stood at attention, hard and pulsing. He smelled sweet with a mixture of syrup and sweat, and his body was at full attention. Marlon stood up and lightly tugged the end of the belt and led her from the kitchen to the bedroom. She followed him to the bedroom, slinking on her hands and knees. Sky stayed on her knees and Marlon pulled the strap tighter towards his body. She quickly kissed the tip of his hardness and then slowly ran her tongue down and up his shaft. She gagged when her mouth reached the end of his shaft, but she did not retreat. She continuously gagged herself until his entire manhood was covered with her sticky saliva. She blew bubbles on the tip and slurped all of it back up again. Marlon was rock hard at the sound of her gagging and slurping. Sky continuously moved up and down between shaft and balls and Marlon heard her say, "I can suck you all day." Marlon's mouth was dry as he watched his manhood disappear behind her soft wet lips.

Sky promised, "You can kill me in this apartment and choke me out if you want. I trust you. Yes, baby. All day. Don't rush. There's no time limit. I'll suck it as nasty and as long as you want me to." His eyes were heavy, and his breathing was slow. She tried to fit both of his balls into her mouth. Then she played with the tip and moved her spit in and out of her mouth like a hissing snake and rubbed his erect penis all over her face.

"Oh shit," He said with an intense whisper.

"I'm not scared to give it all to you," he heard her say. Her lips were soft, and her tongue was unpredictable. She got up off the floor and playfully climbed on the bed. He was right behind her holding her from behind and rubbing his hands around her waist and kissed the back of her ear. "Repeat after me," she said. As she directed his hands to her nipples. He started to play with her hard nipples and was eager to do whatever she said. She put her face in the pillow and spread her cheeks open. "Look at it!" she instructed. He bent her over to see the beauty inside. He inspected her plumpness and parted her lips with his fingers to see the dark pink of the inside of her womanhood peeking at him.

Marlon did not hold back anymore. He entered her and felt the heat to match his heat, slippery wetness, suction, every perfection, and curve inside of her. His thrust was met with grip, contractions, and her rhythm backing up on him. He heard himself say, "You're so wet. You feel so good to me." Her wetness and the smell of her sweat drove him crazy. He pulled out and tried to slow the sex down because he did not want to cum yet.

"Can I have it?" He asked.

"Yes," she responded.

"Are you gonna let me do anal?" He asked in an erotic whisper. The way he said it drove her crazy. She turned around and gave him the devious smile he loved, followed by a kiss. She stood to her feet and walked over to the dresser where she had a drink waiting. She gave him one shot of bourbon. He drank it and then handed him the row of balls connected by a string. Then she gave him an air kiss and another shot of bourbon.

"Do you trust me?" He asked her.

"Yes, I trust you," Sky responded. He poured more than a shot of bourbon into her glass. After she drank it, he turned her around, led her back to the bed, and positioned her on her knees. He pushed the first two balls on the chain into her rectum slowly.

"Is that ok?" Marlon asked.

"Yes, baby, I trust you," Sky confirmed. He slowly pushed in the next two.

"I can take it," she reassured. He slowly slid the small beads in and out and rubbed her nipples. She felt intoxicated as he kissed her back and caressed her nipples as he slid the bigger balls in and out. Her sultry low voice now became a higher pitched, breathy moan that drove him crazy. She was completely prepared for him.
The smooth beads felt good sliding in and out of her rectum. He slowly pushed and pulled the beads in out and replaced them with his fingers. When he was able to put two fingers in her, he knew it was time to enter.

"Baby, do you feel me inside of you?" He heard himself call her 'Baby.' Just as he thought they were on the edge of the world, she took him a little further. He heard her say.

"Put one finger in my ass and the other inside of my pussy and let your fingers touch."

Her nasty instructions sent his mind to another place. He wanted to be inside of her again. His penis was so big Sky wasn't sure if he could fit in her rectum, but she was determined to take it.

"Yes, I can take it," she said. Scared and excited at the same time, she was about to do something new like bungee jumping. Sky could feel the tip of his penis throbbing as he entered her. Sky felt pressure and a little pain at first, followed by heat, and then it turned into pleasure like relieving herself in the bathroom. She was so tight he pushed more of himself in and watched himself sink in slowly like quicksand. It felt like his whole body was inside out!

He watched her beautiful body and Sky's booty jiggled as he stroked in and out from behind her. He squeezed her small waist and thick legs as the sound of her moans danced around his ears. Her chocolate skin had no blemishes and was soft like silk. The aroma of syrup, sweat, bourbon, salt, fire, and excitement was in the air.

Flashes of the candles in the room and the bed beneath them seemed to disappear. They were off the grid, trapped in some kind of time warp or alternate universe. Everything moved in slow motion. He turned her over and put both of her feet over his shoulders. He listened to the sound of her anklet jingle while he was stroking inside of her . Her eyes started rolling in her head as he put one hand around her neck and felt her pulse beating fiercely in the palm of his hands.  Sky spread her legs open to show him his own movements going in and out. The image pushed his senses over the edge and right before he was getting ready to release himself, she screamed in ecstasy, "Marlon!" and coated his phallus with what felt like warm okra.

"Skit?!" Marlon growled and felt himself leave his body and enter hers.

The day had already turned into night. They lay in the bed unable to move for a long time. Marlon was on top and Sky lay beneath him. His head was on her breast as their sweat blended together. Marlon's heat subsided and all their energy, stress, and worries were gone. There was only breathing in the room now. She felt her sweat drying and smelled Marlon's body. He flipped her over on top of him and the sheets beneath them and the air in the room were damp. He rubbed his hand down her back. She let herself feel the calluses on his hand and it felt so good to her. He lay on his back and then motioned for her lips to come to him. She kissed him softly and rubbed the tip of his penis so gently it was sensitive and felt like heaven as they both drifted into sleep.

What they did not know was that unseen spirits joined them. The spirits came one by one with the knowledge of experience and memories. An orgy of emotions, habits, lies, love, lust, confusion, and heartache all laid on top of each other. All the people they slept with in the past, including the people those people slept with and the people those people slept with, totaled two hundred fifty spirits to be exact.

Marlon woke up to a warm cloth wiping his body. First his chest, then his face.

"Skit, what time is it?" He asked with his eyes closed.

"It's about eleven," she responded.

"Let's take a shower," he said.

Sky loved looking in Marlon's eyes in the shower. Marlon knew how to put Sky back together. Marlon took care to wash her back because he knew she liked to be touched there. The water fell on his head, face, lips, and down his chin. Marlon washed her body, and she washed his.

When they finished, Marlon and Sky playfully dried each other, and he lifted her up and carried her to the room, and laid her on the bed. He rubbed her body with her favorite lotion and massaged her feet. Sky fell asleep while he was massaging her. Marlon finished getting dressed, kissed her, and locked the door on his way out.

## 2

## The Maker's House

The next morning Sky did not feel sober. She never felt sober after being with Marlon. She loved being with him. She felt the plush bed under her back, and the comforter rubbed against her breast. She turned her head to the right towards a pillow that still smelled like Marlon. She allowed herself a moment to inhale his smell before opening her eyes. The sound of the alarm on her phone interrupted the quietness of the room. She sat up in bed and scanned her phone for missed calls, text messages, and emails. She slid out of bed and felt the cool fall air in the room.  Everything was illuminated. She sucked her tongue and rubbed the goose bumps that rose on her arms.

As she walked over to the closet to select her clothes, her mind flashed back to the kisses, sounds, and moans of the previous afternoon. Marlon's lips left invisible stains and trails all over her body that could not be washed by the shower. As she made her morning coffee, she stared at the spot on the table where they sexed and decided to eat in the same spot.

In the shower, she remembered the way his eyes felt on her body, and the sensation of soapy bubbles sliding down her back were magnified. She inhaled the steam and held it in as long as she could. She ran her fingertips along the cold tiles of the shower wall in the bathroom as she touched them, she knew sight, sound, touch, and taste were stimulated and heightened. She allowed herself a moment to sit on the bench in her bathroom. That was the only moment of solitude she would probably have all day.  She caught a glimpse of herself in the mirror and thought for one quick second that she saw someone else in her image. She looked again but nothing.  She smiled to herself and wrote it off as just another one of the many heightened sensations and decided to wear her white skirt suit with pearls that day.

She placed her outfit out on the bed. She always loves to wear white after being with Marlon because she felt a need for purification after all the dirty things they did. She applied lotion to her body, pulled on her panties, and sat on the bed staring into space while she finished her coffee. She put on her bra followed by her cream negligée. She pulled on her skirt and looked in the mirror. She pinned her long locks into a bun. She glanced at the time and started to speed up a little. Sky reached for her foundation and caressed her face with the brush in circular motions. She added her suit jacket and brown leather flesh-colored heels. She turned around in the mirror looking herself up and down. She pushed her face close to the mirror and applied the lip liner pencil and then the lipstick.  She stood up straight and practiced her serious face so that nobody would see the insecurity beneath the power suit. Finally, she grabbed her keys and a stack of folders and headed to the car.

The group's Executive Assistant, Sharon, was the first text that came through on Sky's phone followed by what seemed like a tidal wave of violent dings, signaling something was happening. Sky was trying to read Sharon's text while fighting the traffic between her house in Charlestown and the State House. The first text was accompanied by an attachment. Sharon usually waited until Sky responded to her text before calling but as Sky was trying to read the message Sharon was calling her.

"Did you get my message?" Sharon asked with urgency in her tone.

"I'm driving! I was trying to read it when you called." Sky responded.

Sharon's voice was filled with heaviness. Sharon reported. "Preston Johnson passed away at the house. They discovered him this morning."

"What!" Sky responded. Sky felt something leave her body. She was trying to make sure she was hearing Sharon correctly. "Am I hearing you clearly? Did you say Preston died?" She felt hot tears well up and blinked profusely to stop the tears from falling.

"Yes, they just discovered him about thirty minutes ago," Sharon confirmed with sadness.

Sky commanded. "I'll be there in ten minutes. Send someone out to park my car."

"Drive up to the front and James will park for you." Sharon confirmed.

Sky felt the high intoxicating feeling from being with Marlon go away immediately as she pulled in front of the building and exchanged places with James. She almost ran from her car into the building. As the elevator rose higher and higher to the third floor, she felt her heart beating, her mouth watering as if she was going to vomit, and her stomach tightened. Sky was greeted with a wall of silence and eyes that saw her and quickly looked away as she walked from the elevator to her office. Sharon entered right behind her and turned on the television to the news.

"Preston Johnson was found mutilated and non-responsive this morning at The Maker's House. The Maker's House is known as an alternative home for children while their parents are treated for mental health issues. There are not many details available. Our team will be reporting as this story unfolds. Stay tuned, we will keep you posted."

Sky shouted at the TV in anger, "How did they get that information? Aren't kids supposed to have confidentiality?"

Sharon told Sky, "I will get every single detail I can get for you. I already have the staff sign-in sheets from the last six months and the names of all the kids who were on site."

Sky interrupted, "Thank you. I also want updated criminal background checks from the last six months of all staff. Please call the staff that was on duty and tell them to fax us the visitor logs and instruct them not to comment about what happened to anyone."

"Sure thing!" Sharon responded.

"I also need to know all of the details of what happened," Sky added.

"Ok, I'll be back shortly," Sharon guaranteed. Sharon closed the door behind her and left Sky alone. Sky drifted into a plethora of emotions. The Maker's House was Sky's personal project. It was supposed to provide a haven for children, and now children were being killed in the very place they were supposed to be safe. Sky's thoughts became fierce and deeply focused. She clenched her hands into a tight fist and walked back and forth. She blew air in and out to try to calm herself, but it was not working.

Sky began to struggle mentally and attempted to push back the memories of when she was a foster child. The memories were overpowering as Sky recalled the faces and fake smiles of her abusers who only wanted a check for flesh and didn't care about her or the other kids they fostered. She was determined to stay in the present moment. Sky personally raised the funds. She organized fundraisers and community feedback sessions where she had to smile when she did not want to smile. She wrote grants and personally convinced constituents, funders, the Mayor, the Governor, and anyone else of the importance for children with parents with mental illness to have a safe place to live while their parents were in treatment.

The Maker's House was a temporary home. She reassured the community that the kids would be safe with the goal of reunification with their parents. She was elected to office as a State Representative, a fierce advocate, and a protector of children. The file about Preston was on her desk with his picture on the cover. The beautiful eight-year-old, with big eyes and a sweet smile, was found dead at the House. Sky then remembered how she was taken from her mother when she was eight.

Sky tried to stay focused on the present moment. She had not thought about her childhood for years. Her heartbeat was quickening. "Think fast. Think fast. Keep your head in the game," she told herself. Sky wanted to cry. She tried to regain her composure as saliva flooded her mouth and she quickly grabbed her waste-paper basket and threw up. The Maker's House was the most important thing to Sky. She was determined to change the outcome of violence, the heightened chance of incarceration, and the suicide rate of aged-out kids. But on that day, she failed.  She kept staring at the beautiful boy and his big smile.

She knew that all eyes would be on her and she tried to regain her composure.  She took very good care to always have on pressed clothes, make-up, regal posture, high heels, leather bags, manicured nails, and beautifully sculpted hair. These things helped her hide the vulnerable little girl she used to be, but none of it could help her now. She detested when people's eyes would stare at her because it evoked feelings from her childhood.  She remembered people gawking at her and her mother all the time.

Sky's mother never received a proper diagnosis for her mental illness and for many years it was undetected. When people finally realized something was wrong, it was ignored. The outbursts reached a critical point that could no longer be ignored.  At first, they called her mother's mental illness manic depression, followed by bipolar and finally paranoid schizophrenia. The various medications were like a parade that bombarded Sky's life. As a little child, she had no idea anything was wrong. She did not know that people turned the lights off at night while sleeping.  She thought everyone placed water in every room, a pile of rocks on the names of perceived enemies, a line of cayenne pepper and salt behind every door. Sky considered it good fun to paint their doors and window sills blue. Her mother walked through the streets with a shopping cart collecting cans and panhandling on corners. Sky's mother always refused to work because she wanted to be with Sky. Her mother would declare, "God will provide." They had a small corner devoted to giving instructions to angels that were supposed to be for her protection. Her mother would always say, "Ministering angels please today make sure you keep the spirits away."

The final straw was when a woman on the street dressed in all red and a hat with a veil tried to touch Sky. Her mother physically assaulted her with punches, kicks, and lastly a rock. Sky's mother chanted, "I ain't scared. I ain't scared. I ain't scared." She instructed Sky to run home and hide. The police arrested her mom, and her mother was admitted to the hospital. Sky was left in the house for three days by herself before it was discovered in her mother's evaluation that she had a child. The police arrived at the house, and Sky was asleep under the bed with the lights on. The officers arrived with a woman in a pantsuit who asked, "What is your name? When was the last time you ate? Does your mom hit you?" Sky answered honestly not knowing that telling the stranger about the angels, rituals, and diet were all securing that fact that she would never see her home or her mother again.

She was sent to an emergency site and everything was foreign to her. The first night in the group home was cold. The room they gave her had a hard mattress and rough, hard itchy wool comforter with a hard pillow that felt like a dried-out sponge. The room smelled like old milk, sweat, and urine. The first night was scary and Sky cried thinking about her mother and what would happen to her. She had no idea where her mother was, and no one explained what was happening. She wondered for weeks about her mother as she stared at the cinder block walls with light green paint while sitting on the hard furniture.

Although her mother had issues, Sky always felt loved. She missed the Saturday morning pancakes and cleaning marathon in which her mother cleaned and organized everything for hours to the sound of gospel music. Her mother gave her continuous hugs and asked where she was going several times a day. Her mother was undoubtedly a good woman even though she struggled with reality. She inspected her food and looked in every room before Sky would enter. She double-checked bags as if she were expecting something to be hiding inside. Sky felt safe with her mother which was contrary to what she was told. According to her caseworker, her mother was a danger to herself and Sky.

Sky did not hear from her mother until five months later when she showed up at Sky's new school screaming her name in the hallway. Sky was excited to hear her mother's voice that day and ran to meet her. Her presence caused a commotion as the teachers and Principal explained to her that she could not see Sky. Sky ran to her mother only to be kept apart by more and more teachers. Sky's mother started reaching furiously to reach Sky and then the reaching turned into swinging punches at the school staff. The police arrived and the officers held her mother down as she screamed until her voice had no more sound.

Sky was embarrassed, scared, and did not know what to do. The kids were kept in their classrooms, but the word was out that Sky's mother was "crazy". The story was passed around and Sky spent the rest of her school career making herself invisible. The next time she heard about her mother was six months after that incident. It was confirmed her mom was being admitted into the women's State prison for women that committed crimes. Her mother's mental health was evaluated by the criminal justice system. Sky was also sentenced to cold Christmas holidays in group homes wondering who she was and where she came from and why that was happening. She knew she had to have come from somewhere, and Sky imagined perhaps she had grandmothers, brothers, or sisters.  However, it was just her mother and her in this terrible situation.

She was nine when she was completely crushed by loneliness and realized no one was ever coming. She had to rescue herself.  Sky decided to be an excellent student. It did not matter that her first foster home locked her in the closet for months and the father, mother, and brother of that home raped her. She studied and read and became mentally strong and sober and powerful, emotionless, and that was the woman she needed at this moment.

The Maker's House was her attempt to stop kids from feeling what she felt. The house was supposed to resemble Miss Ma Jessie's house. The first foster home that she ever felt protected and loved. All her money, time, and late nights were dedicated to this house. The rooms were filled with books and lamps with soft beds and music. The evaluators were trained to talk with warmth and concern. The social workers were given the history of the children and trained to handle them with dignity, respect, and humanity.  The questions in her mind were, *"Who would do this to children?"* and *"How could this happen with all the precautions taken?"*  Sky believed in her heart that she had to go through those things so that she could help other kids and stop them from going through what she had gone through.

Her thoughts were interrupted by Sharon's knock on the door. Sharon entered with fresh hot coffee. Her presence snapped Sky out of her trance. Sharon explained that the Governor and the Mayor wanted an emergency meeting before they spoke to the District Attorney's office. They demanded an explanation as to why a child was able to be mutilated to death under the watchful eye of the State.

Sharon looked shaken. She sat uncomfortably close to Sky and brought her voice down to a very low whisper so only the two of them could hear. She began, "I called my detective friend. We are not supposed to know any of this information. You must keep this between us until the police and the district attorney release the information to you.

Preston was in the middle of the circle. There were eight children around him. He was sliced with razor blades until he bled to death. They said there was no struggle though. The other kids also had slices on their bodies. Some of their wounds were healed and some wounds were fresh like they were doing a ceremony. They did the ceremony during a shift change. The night staff was ending, and the morning staff was coming on. The morning staff went to check their rooms.

They started from the first floor and went up. It probably took them thirty minutes to get to the third floor. When the staff got up to the third floor, none of the kids on the third floor were there. They found the kids in the basement's common room where they were all lethargic and sliced."

Sky could not believe what Sharon was telling her. She stared at Sharon for a few seconds. Sky was thankful to Sharon. She could not imagine facing this day without her. Sharon was in her mid-forties but looked thirty. Her face was kind and her patience unmatched. Her kind eyes were welcomed at that moment. She handed Sky the statements from the staff, criminal background checks, and schedules she asked for earlier. They sat in her office and went over the details.  The morning was gone and the day approached evening.

Sky told Sharon to prepare everyone for a meeting. She put her coffee on the desk and took five minutes to review the statement that she already started preparing in her head after Sharon's messages were sent to her phone. Sky could see people scrambling to the meeting. She composed a list of people to be questioned immediately by the district attorney because they may have known about the abuse and she wanted to reassure the public that something was being done. As she walked into the meeting everyone was silent. She started reading her statement as soon as she walked into the room. "The details of what happened are currently being investigated by law enforcement. All records regarding the Maker's House staff have been released to detectives and the district attorney's office to ensure a thorough investigation. We would like to extend our deepest apologies and condolences to the families of the children." She gave the names on her list to the department heads for them to begin the process of cleaning up. The meeting was full of schedule and video surveillance reviews, the chain of events leading up to his death, and all the case details with names, dates, times, and incident reports. The attorneys advised Sky how to proceed, so she instructed the receptionist to send the statement to the paper. Sky's meeting ended at 7:30 p.m., and her experience with Marlon was not only a distant memory but not important at all.

She turned on the television at 9:00 p.m. to view the breaking news and listened as they released the statement she prepared with her staff. After the breaking news statement aired, Sky's phone rang, and the Governor was

on the line. She held her breath. She knew the only reason
she could possibly be receiving a call from the Governor
was that heads were about to roll or more specifically her
head was about to roll. State representatives received calls
from constituents demanding answers and justice. In turn,
they pressured and urged the Governor to personally seek
answers. The story reached a national level, so Preston
Johnson's face, Massachusetts, and the Maker's House
made national news. The words that the Governor spoke
to Sky, faded as she could not believe what was happening.
All she remembered was they were filled with spice and
tension. Sky felt stripped bare. She had done a lot to
escape criticism by working hard for everything and
avoiding errors. The Governor's lecture and scolding left
her feeling weak, empty, and helpless. He demanded to
hear her plan. She explained the task force that she had
set up, her plan of action, and people who had already
been referred to the district attorney for questioning. Her
report was thorough and detailed. He was annoyed but
satisfied.

As he spoke, she scanned her perfect office for dust or
anything that was out of place so she could fix it. Her office
was perfect with the white leather chair, the glass desktop,
to the crystal that lined the windowsill. She kicked herself
for not personally overseeing the site visitations. She
reviewed the list of staff names.

*Dr. Stacy Wilson*
*Deborah Jenkins*
*Dr. Katherine O'Connor*
*Sandra Smith*
*Elizabeth Steele*
*Donna Stevenson*
*Dr. Abishai Malcam*

*Billy Canton*
*Brittany Sledge*
*William Murphy*
*Divine Brown*

Sky left the office at 10:00 p.m. and did not acknowledge her staff. She wanted to get out of there as quickly as possible. No one on the staff would dare move a muscle or leave before her. She walked out of the door and was only comforted by the distorted reflection of herself in the elevator dressed in a beautiful stark white outfit. She tried her best to numb herself and not feel the crushing loneliness that was her constant companion.

In the car, she thought about the kids at the house. She wondered where they would go and what they would do when the funding was pulled. She thought about Marlon as she drove home. He called her five times and texted her three times. Sky entered her apartment exhausted and glad to be home.  She turned the hallway light on and walked down the hallway, taking off her coat and shoes, and placing them in the closet. She commanded, "Kitchen light on. Play something soft!" As she walked to the kitchen. She scanned her wines and filled her glass with merlot. She filled her glass again, again, again, and again. She sat with her fingertips touching, eyes closed, and breathing deeply before she got up to walk into her bedroom.  Her phone was on silent but the screen lit up and the name read Miss Jessie. The call Sky could not refuse.

"Hello," Miss Jessie said softly when Sky picked up. Sky could not respond because tears choked her.

"Sky?" Miss Jessie questioned.

"Yes, Miss Jessie" Sky responded through her tears.

"I saw da news and I just want to let you know don't feel bad for doing the right thing. I'm proud of you baby. I know it's late but I just want to let you know that you will be ok." Miss Jessie reassured.

"Miss Jessie, I did everything in my power to prevent something like this from happening. I just don't understand." Sky expressed with dejection in her voice.

"Everything is not always understood the moment it happens. Sometimes understanding is for the future. Make sure you take it easy on yourself. I know how you are. Don't be over there beating yourself up for things that are out of your control." Miss Jessie comforted me.

"I want kids to feel protected the way you made us feel. I want to keep building what you started. I don't want to let you down" Sky explained.

"NEVER!" Miss Jessie cut her off.

"You could NEVER let me down. All the mountains you have climbed!"

Sky sniffled and said, "Thank you, Miss Jessie."

"I know you have a lot going on, but I want to see you ok?" Miss Jessie requested.

"Ok" Sky responded.

After talking with Miss Jessie. Sky sat in silence drinking her wine while staring into space as she thought about Preston and his last moments. Suddenly, the hair on the back of her neck slowly stood up, and she sensed someone watching her. Her eyes walked around the apartment fiercely. Everything was in perfect order. The perfume bottles on the dresser were perfectly lined from smallest to largest. The sheets on the bed were pristine white and crisp and the pillows were arranged like dominoes. No dust lingered in any corner, nor did any stray crumb linger. The wooden floorboards glistened. The cleanliness made the loft apartment seem even larger. She scanned the couch with her eyes and quickly turned because she sensed movement behind her. She turned around and found nothing. "Perhaps the wine is taking its effect," Sky said out loud. She began to stare left too long and stared right too long, and then she spotted the baby gnat.

Suddenly she saw two, then three, and then the gnats started to flood the apartment. They landed on everything in sight. Sky was shocked as she swatted at the swarm. She started moving quickly to her phone to call someone. She reached for the phone, but it disappeared.

The walls turned green, and her beautiful hardwood floor turned into brown, muddy dirt below. Sky tried to close her eyes. But whether her eyes were closed or open, she could not tell because the motion did not change the fact that her house was turning into a forest. She breathed in and out, in and out, and she saw her mirror. That was the only part of her house that was left. She ran to the mirror. Sky caught the mirror with her eyes and noticed someone was standing directly behind her. She thought it was her reflection, but it was a woman.

Her heart felt as if it was dropped into a frying pan. The room became smaller and black as she turned to face the intruder, and the floor began rushing towards her.

Sky lay on the floor overwhelmed and exhausted by fear. The books on the shelves and the clocks on the wall watched as Baby Gnats emerged. The room was spinning, spinning, spinning. Sky confirmed to herself, "I think I'm drunk."

### 3
### Visions during the day


The next morning Sky was awakened by her speeding heart. *What a dream* she thought to herself. She was cold and could not catch her breath right away. She sat up to drink water and realized she was in her bed still fully dressed. She could not remember how she made it to bed. Her head was pounding, and she did not want to face the day. Stomach quivering, she rubbed her face and tried to comfort herself. "Five more minutes to hide," she said out loud. She closed her eyes to give herself a moment only to be interrupted by the sonar sound alarm. The sound was supposed to gradually increase naturally and slowly, but Sky was annoyed. She got out of bed and rushed through her morning routine to get out of the door and face the day. Shower, coffee, check phone clothes, makeup, check phone, shoes, jewelry, hair, sunglasses, check phone, lock door, drive, check the phone. When she arrived at work she was greeted by reporters in the front, and she was thankful that there was a staff door she could enter through. High heels echoing on the marble floor, she walked down the hall to her office. The marble floor made her feel even more lonely. "BUZZZZ, BUZZZZ," her phone vibrated. Marlon sent her a text. "There's a muffin and orange juice waiting for you on your desk!" The message made her smile, eased her a little, and made it possible to walk the rest of the seventy-five feet to her desk. The staff was talking but fell silent when she entered. A few quiet good mornings rang in the air. Sky returned the greetings with a dry, "Hello." She did not want to sound too cozy as she needed them to be alert.

She felt relieved to be in her office. She looked in the mirror on her desk to refresh her foundation as sweat was forming on her upper lip and nose. She checked her face for eyeliner errors and any other imperfections. The huge blueberry muffin from her favorite café greeted her. She put the muffin in her mouth and tasted the tart contrasting the sweet perfectly as she thought to herself, '*I'm really hungry.*" The orange juice was so cold it was sweating on her desk. She picked it up and gulped it down and stared out of the window at the pigeons on the ledge. She tried to organize her day. Messages, emails, meetings, lunch, she thought. "You have twelve new messages," was the response after she pressed the envelope button on her phone. Message one, "My name is Rachel Smith, and I'm calling because my daughter was in the house. Can you please call me back? Sky pressed skip. Message two, I am trying to reach State Rep Sky Jones. I'm calling from NEWS wonder. I have some questions from your constituents, and they would love to hear a response from you. Can you please…" Sky pressed skip.  Her inbox was full of messages about Preston. Her hands started to shake as she listened.

She closed her eyes for a moment and when she opened them Sky watched her beautiful office turn into a horizon of red dirt. She saw a woman run by in terror. As the woman ran past her, she was filled with the same fear and breathlessness as the running woman. Sky began panting and sweating. She tried to see who was chasing her but could only see what was in front. She grabbed the arms of the chair in her office real tight and wondered if it was all real. She found herself inhaling red dirt. She was interrupted by a gentle touch on her shoulder. Sky was glad to see Sharon standing over her and talking to her. "Are you ok?" Sharon asked. The woman who was running disappeared. "Don't worry about what's happening. Everything will blow over as soon as the next big news story comes along." Sharon confirmed.

Sky placed her hand on Sharon's arm ever so lightly and said, "Please don't go yet."

Sharon was happy to stand by her side. "What's wrong?" Sharon asked. Sky decided to ask Sharon questions related to the case just so she would not have to feel those feelings and see those visions.

"Nothing, have you heard anything else from your friend?" Sky asked with urgency.

"Yes, he said they can't really find any signs of foul play from any adults. All of the kids seemed willing to cut themselves. Everyone on the list is clean so far." Sharon reported. Sky thought to herself, *"How Strange"*

As soon as Sharon left the room, Sky called Dr. Davis. She reviewed the story she was going to tell Dr. Davis in her mind so that she would not seem crazy. She would tell her that she was having dreams and would describe what happened the night before and what happened in the office that morning in detail.

She would not dare tell her that she was experiencing visions in the middle of the day and feeling and seeing things in real-time that were not actually happening currently, but were happening or happened somewhere before.  Sky did not think she would be able to see Dr. Davis, but she was relieved when there was an opening. She spoke to the receptionist and scheduled the appointment. She headed over. Time and space seemed strange. She floated by the people in Boston Common and gave coins to everyone that asked her for money.  She seemed to float over everything as if she were in a time warp. The walk was a short one from the State House to Washington street.

Dr. Davis' office was a refuge of sorts to Sky. The smell of the carpet and books was relaxing. She helped Sky work through so many issues in the past. Dr. Davis greeted Sky and waved her into the office. She opened her arms and hugged Sky.

"Hi, I'm so glad you're here. Please sit down." Sky sat and even though she had been here a million times she still scanned Dr. Davis' huge bookshelf. The books made her feel safe somehow. Sky sat down on the edge of the chair.

"Do you know why I'm here?" Sky asked.

"I've seen the news, but I don't want to assume. Why don't you tell me why you're here?" Dr. Davis said as she leaned closer to Sky.

"So, you know what happened to Preston?" Sky asked.

"Yes, I've heard a little." Dr. Davis responded. Sky felt like she wanted to burst into tears, but she swallowed hard instead.

Dr. Davis asked Sky, "Do you feel anxious?"

"Yes." She said emphatically.

"Let us do a breathing exercise first," the doctor suggested.

"Ok," Sky replied.

Dr. David said, "Close your eyes. Let's breathe in slowly one… two… three… and out one… two… three…
In one… two… three… and out one… two… three… one… two… three… and out one… two… three… one… two… three… and out one… two… three… Now tell me, what are you feeling?"

After breathing Sky began to explain slowly, "I feel responsible for what happened to Preston, you know! I want to do right by these kids. Nobody understands how hard it is for them. I just wanted them to feel safe, loved, and get the services they needed."

"Well, there is no way you could have known what was going to happen." Dr. Davis reassured.

"I know…I feel like I was distracted, and I should have been on top of this." Sky expressed with blame in her voice.

"How were you distracted?" Dr. Davis asked.

"I don't know, spending too much time with Marlon, maybe? Died! A boy actually died! How does that happen? Sky questioned rhetorically.

Dr. Davis stared and listened intensely.

"I am supposed to know how that happens." Sky said as if she was confronting herself.

"There are some things that are beyond our control. It will not help to beat up on yourself. You see yourself in each of these kids and that is why you are being so hard on yourself." Dr. Davis reassured.

Sky said, "I feel like I let so many people down."

"I would like for you to take it easier on yourself because you have done a lot for those children. It is important for us to pause a moment and use one of our tools. We don't want to accept abuse from other people, and we also must be aware not to be abusive to ourselves," Dr. Davis explained.

"Ok." Sky agreed reluctantly.

"So, let us go to the safe house we built for ourselves. Tell me about your safe house," Dr. Davis said.

"Nobody in. Nobody out." Sky said out loud.

"Yes, Nobody in. Nobody out," Dr. Davis repeated after Sky.

"The only person with a key is me. I can be naked; I can be honest because there is nobody there but me." Sky affirmed.

"Yes, let's breathe. Tell me more," the doctor stated.

"I am safe, I am whole, and I am ok," Sky confirmed.

"Yes, that's good stuff." Dr. Davis encouraged. "Now shall we go over some facts?"

"Yes," Sky answered.

Dr. Davis asked, "How many children have you helped in the past five years? Those kids would have been lost in foster care or child services. How many children have you helped be reunited with their families? Take a moment and breathe with me. I want you to answer the questions."

Sky breathed in and out with Dr. Davis. "Let's focus our energy on the positive." the doctor said as she handed Sky a notepad.

"The structure is twenty children at a time and there is no limit on their stay. For five years? I would say about two hundred sixty." Sky confirmed.

"Wow! And that is also the number that would not have been helped if it were not for the Maker's House. I want you to focus on that number two hundred sixty and breathe. I want to give you this number to carry with you and when you start to think of Preston, I want you to acknowledge him, and I also want you to remember the other two hundred sixty souls you have helped. Does that sound like something you can try?" Dr. Davis asked.

"Yes," Sky said, feeling encouraged.

"Tell me more." Dr. Davis inquired.

"I'm having horrible nightmares," Sky confessed.

"Really? What are the dreams about?" the doctor asked.

Sky explained with hesitation. "I keep seeing a woman that I do not know, running. I also had a dream about flies in my apartment and a forest that keeps trying to consume me."

Dr. Davis responded with understanding, "Well, based on everything you're going through, these dreams don't seem unusual. The situation you're in is tough. Anyone would want to run away. You are under a tremendous amount of stress. Let us figure out some strategies to help you cope with the dreams, and also the stress.  I'm going to prescribe you something to help you with the anxiety and to help you calm down."

After seeing Dr. Davis, Sky felt relieved. She walked back to the office. Sharon greeted her as she walked in. Sky settled in and began reading her emails. The complaints started pouring in.

Dear Representative Smith,
I was disappointed to learn of the misfortune at the Maker's House.

Dear Representative Jones,
Children are innocent and you are irresponsible.

Dear Sky Jones,
Blood is on your hands Bitch! You farm kids for your own benefit. What goes around comes around!

Dear Sky,

You take kids from their families and can't even protect them.

Sky logged out of her email and closed her eyes. She started the breathing exercise doctor Davis gave her. "Two hundred sixty" Two hundred fifty-nine, Two hundred fifty-eight, Two hundred fifty-seven. It calmed her. When she opened her eyes, there was a small gnat resting on a banana across the room. Her heart started racing and the office disappeared. "Oh no, Oh no, no, no, no, no!" The desk, chair, and walls were replaced with thick trees and green leaves. The gnats flew towards her and started landing on her body. Sky swatted and yelled, "No, no, no!"

Sharon entered the room and the forest and gnats disappeared. Sharon saw Sky in distress and approached her. Sky grabbed Sharon's arm. "It's ok," Sharon said.
"Something is wrong with me." Sky blurted out.
"Stop blaming yourself! Don't read any more of those emails. I'll read them and respond for you." Sharon demanded.
"No! that's not it!" Sky said and was visibly shaking.
"What's wrong?" Sharon asked.

Sky stared at Sharon as she filtered what to say. She did not want to sound crazy. Sharon locked the door and moved closer to her. "You can tell me!" Sharon convinced. Sky just continued to stare. She could feel her sweat and wiped her face. The brown foundation came off on her hands. She checked her desk for a napkin and a mirror so she could see her face. Sharon sat quietly with concern on her face.

Water started to come to Sky's eyes. "I am so stressed!" Sky managed to say with a crackling voice.

"The things that you and I talk about are between us." Sharon kneeled on the floor in front of Sky and held her shaking hands. "What's wrong?" Sharon asked.

"I don't want you to think I'm crazy." Sharon reminded Sky of her mother at that moment for so many reasons. She was attentive as if Sky were the only person in the world and because Sky's mother was about thirty-five when she had a mental break. Sky started to breathe heavily as if the air in the room was leaving. Sharon started to breathe with her and said, "Calm down. Let's breathe!"

They breathed together and finally, Sky said, "My mother was about my age when she had her nervous breakdown." Sharon squeezed her hands and looked into her face.  Sky held back but Sharon would not allow her to retreat.

"What does that have to do with you?" Sharon asked.

"I think the same thing is happening to me. I am not ok! I'm not ok!" Sky admitted.

Sharon shook her head back and forth gesturing no with her head and said, "Shhhhh, Shhhh, shhhh, shhhh shhhh shhhhh shhhhhh, don't agree with them. Your words are more powerful than you think! What's happening?"

"I am seeing things that aren't there, Sharon! Yesterday when I went home, my apartment changed from a building to a forest and was full of gnats. I woke up in the morning and thought it was a dream, but when I sat in the office this morning, I saw this woman running and it felt like I was running. I went to see Dr. Davis and I took medication, but a few minutes ago, I saw a gnat on that banana and the same thing happened again! This office turned into a forest but this time everything was more vivid than last night. I could smell the trees and the dirt! It is getting worse. I'm scared to be by myself." Sky said as she cried hysterically. Sharon grabbed her and hugged her. Sharon let her cry and then got up and reached for the water on the desk. Sharon wiped Sky's face and said, "Drink this" and handed her the water.

"I don't know what to do. I need help." Sky said desperately.

"Listen, I don't believe you have a physical problem. You have a spiritual problem. Have you ever heard of the woman in the bible with the issue of blood?" Sharon asked.

Sky was relieved that Sharon did not think she was crazy but now was hoping Sharon was not going to use this to preach to her.

"No, I don't read the bible and I never went to church." Sky admitted.

"It sounds to me like you have an issue of blood." Sharon continued, "Do you remember a couple of years ago when I fell ill all of a sudden?"

"Yes," Sky recalled.

"Well, the doctors could not figure out what was wrong with me. I went to the doctor because one morning I woke up and all my joints were hurting. Then my eyesight was attacked, then my lungs. I got progressively worse, and they took all kinds of tests. Lupus, connective tissue disease, etc. Then spots appeared on my lungs and they had to remove a portion of it for my biopsy. The conclusion and diagnosis they presented to me was organized pneumonia. I left the hospital with thirteen medications with the expectation that I would decline in health over the years. The medications did not help me.

One night I felt a presence over me as I lay in bed. I looked up and it began to smother me. I thought I was dreaming, and I could not tell if I was awake or if it was real. My body was weak, but I fought off the presence. I was so scared after that night.

Then, one day I was in Codman Square walking and this man passed me. And when he passed me, it felt like a shock or charge of energy hit my body. He looked at me and I looked at him and he said, 'There's something following you.' I started crying right away. He told me to come to his store. I went and if you could imagine I did what they told me to do, and I was free. I have no more medications and the doctors are shocked by how my condition was reversed. I know what you're telling me is real and I don't think you're crazy at all." Sharon confirmed.

Sky looked at Sharon with relief.

"Do you think he can help me?" Sky asked.

"If they can't help you, no one can." Sharon responded with certainty.

<u>4</u>
<u>Not Today</u>

The store was stark white in a field with nothing on the left or right side. It was made from brick and shorter than the buildings that were being constructed down the street. A heavy metal gate with several locks guarded the entrance.

Sky read the sign of this broken-down store on the building as they entered. It read *The King of Love*. Sky stood behind Sharon and thought it would be best for Sharon to do all the talking. Sharon sat down quietly on the cracked leather sofa and Sky followed her lead. She whispered to Sharon, "How ridiculous, is the store completely unattended?" Sharon was quiet and uninterested in Sky's small talk.

Sky scanned the room looking at candles, books, nails, saints, oils, and jars that appeared to be filled with nothing but dirt. Finally, an old man emerged. Sharon stood in his presence and Sky delayed standing. Sky was freaked out by his eyes which seemed to be covered with a white and gray film. Sharon presented him with apples, pears, and six yards of material that were neatly wrapped inside of her bag. The old man almost cracked a smile until he saw Sky. Sharon was always polite and professional but today she was even more gracious. She was full of gestures such as palm over the chest and slight bows, the kind of respect Sky had not seen in years. "Uncle Love, this is my boss Sky Jones."

Sky interrupted, "Good evening" and extended her hand. Uncle did not extend his hand in return. Sky was not sure if he could see her hand or if he were just rude and refused to touch her hand. They heard someone else walk up the stairs. Sky could not see the young woman clearly as she passed by the room. The old man commanded, "Solace, guard your gates." On cue, the young woman left faster than she came.

Love started walking to a back room. Sharon smiled at Sky and motioned her slightly, and Sky took a deep breath. Sharon knew to follow Love into the side room. He pushed back the old-fashioned green beaded curtain and slowly took a seat. Sharon sat on the small armchair off to the side that was not placed at the table. The only seat left was the one directly across from Uncle Love. The table had a light that hung over it, and Sky was able to see his whole face and grayish-white eyes.

Uncle didn't say anything. He just picked the teapot off the table and slowly poured the amber liquid into a cup. The steam released a cinnamon ginger aroma into the room. He did not offer Sky or Sharon anything to drink. Sky cleared her throat and adjusted her body, not sure of what to do next.

Love asked, "What have you seen?" Sky did not know what to say or how much she should reveal to this Uncle Love. She knew that telling people about visions in the middle of the day, heart palpitations, and talking about things that other people could not see was trouble. Sharon sensed her reluctance and offered to excuse herself so that she could speak freely. "Sky, I'll be right in the front if you want more privacy or if you need me."

"No, I may need you to remind me if I forget something," Sky said as she placed her hand on Sharon's shoulder.

Love looked at Sky and thought to himself, *all of God's most beautiful browns were laid on this woman.* Her skin was deep, dark, and smooth with no blemishes. She had warm mahogany with sepia undertones. The light revealed that her big beautiful almond-shaped eyes were dark molasses colored with black ebony rings in the center and polished like candy. Her lips were the color of coffee beans full and moist. The shape resembled the arches and dips of a graceful bird in flight with wings fully extended. Her long lashes were chocolate-colored and hypnotizing with each blink. Her copper-colored locks fell right above her waist and it was as if even her hair thought she was beautiful.

The creases in her clothes were so sharp that Love could not find one piece of lint or imperfection. Her lacquered nails, gold jewelry, the straight lines of her eyeliner, and the aroma of her soft leather purse were nothing and seemed silly in comparison to the beautiful browns God layered on Sky. Sky prepared to edit herself.

"I have been under a lot of pressure lately because of the various projects that I oversee at my office. A young boy was found unresponsive by one of the staff members at the house that I started for children whose parents are struggling with mental illness. We were supposed to protect children like him. It's hard for me to watch the news because I see his face. This situation is causing me to lose sleep. When I do sleep, I am having weird dreams. I see a young woman, corridors, rooms, and I am not sure what all of this means." Sky said reluctantly.

Uncle closed his eyes as if he were digesting the information that she gave him. The room fell silent for about thirty seconds before Love asked the next question. "What have you eaten?"

"What have I been eating?" Sky repeated.

"Yes, what have you been eating?" Love asked again.

"It's very hard for me to eat right now. I usually have the same thing every day: coffee for breakfast, a salad for lunch, and usually chicken or fish for dinner." Sky said with annoyance in her voice.

"Is there a reason why you always have the same thing?" Love asked. Sky thought about the home she came from and how there were no scheduled eating times. Love added to the question. "Do you ever eat things prepared by other people?"

"Almost all my food is prepared by other people." Sky said matter of factly.

"Humph," Love exclaimed, "what have you heard?" love asked.

"I've been hearing the news. People are outraged by Preston's death." Sky answered.

"Most importantly, who have you been having sex with?" Love asked unapologetically. Sky became extremely uncomfortable with that question and looked at Sharon.

"Is this a joke?" Sky asked. "I think that question is too personal. I don't know what that has to do with what I am here for. I think that's out of line." Love detected an increase in emotion and defensiveness and a need to protect this information. Sky declared, "There are some questions I am not going to answer because they are too personal."

"You have not answered any questions since you started speaking. These are all surface answers," Love reassured. "

"I just don't see how these questions are going to help me!" Sky barked.

Love intensely responded, "If you want to find out what is happening to you, I need you to tell me the truth." Sky paused as she tried to figure out whether to filter or tell Love what was really happening to her. Sharon seemed annoyed with her reluctance and interjected, "She keeps seeing a woman running."

Love repeated, "Running? When you see someone running, that is serious business. I suggest you get *real*, real quick.  The choice is yours." Love's words released a warning.

Sky looked at Love and thought to herself, *What am I doing here?* She also decided at that moment that she was never coming back to this store, this man, or his daughter. Sky started to stand as she said, "Thank you for your time, Mister." With sarcasm in her tone, she squinted with her eyes and waited for him to fill in his full name.  He stared at her with a look of annoyance.

At that moment, Solace reappeared in the doorway. Love said, "I want you to talk to my daughter because I can't help you if you don't want to help yourself. Maybe you will feel more comfortable with these kinds of questions. I don't know what you think you came here for but this is not a joke." Sky looked at Solace and thought how this stylish young woman looked out of place in this old store.

Sky stood and marched out of the room. "I'm leaving," she said to Sharon.

Sharon hugged Love and said, "Thank you for your time, Uncle."

In the car, Sky asked Sharon, "What was he, some voodoo doctor or something? These people find out a few facts about a person, put two and two together, and come up with creative ways to get money out of you. No thanks! I'll pass! I am all set!"

"I think you should give yourself a chance, Sharon responded.

Sky asked, "What was that you gave him? Did you pay him?"

Sharon said, "I gave him respect and a small token of appreciation for seeing you. Sharon was very quiet as she checked her phone for missed calls and emails and then calmly told Sky, "I don't believe that Sky, but I do believe that if nothing spiritual is happening then you will be fine. If there is something spiritual happening, then these are the people you want to help you. They are not voodoo or witch doctors. They are Christians and they are Prophets"

"I am all set!" Sky retorted.

Sharon remembered what Love told her in the past about people. He said, "A person has to make the decision to be helped by helping themselves. You can't help someone that does not want to change. You can't want something for a person they don't want for themselves." Sharon changed the subject for the drive back to the office.

Love and Solace sat to discuss the encounter. He told Solace, "The woman who came here today withheld and lied to us, but she lied to herself too. She will return when the need for the truth becomes unbearable. The gates are open on this one. She came in with both angels, and demons, and she is battling herself."

Solace knew what that meant. Love taught her in the past that spiritual things enter through gates. Guard what you see. Guard what you hear. Guard what comes out of your mouth, Solace recalled. Love told her in the past that you can tell what people allowed into their gates by what comes out of their mouths.

"Did you pray and ask the Lord for protection?" Love asked.

"Yes, as soon as you told me," Solace confirmed.

"The demon, 'Baby Gnats', is assigned to her, and some other spirit," Love confirmed.

"What kind of demon is 'Baby Gnats'?" Solace asked.

Love explained. "BABY Gnats is a small demon that comes when many spirits summon its presence. 'Baby Gnats' is one of the worst kinds of demons. It is easily underestimated because of its small size. However, this kind of demon can multiply and infest the host at a high speed. It can make connections with other spirits and demons and reproduce and attract so many of them until they form one unified powerful nagging demon. Usually, there are many vices and ties involved if someone has the demon 'baby gnats.' If spirits were detecting trauma, dishonesty, sex, and love, then they would summon that demon.

Solace asked, "What is the difference between a spirit and a demon?"

"Spirits are the energy of people that have actually existed on the earth before. If humans die, that previous energy remains on earth if their spirit is not settled for some reason. All spirits are not bad but if they are bad or were bad all the grossness from that spirit still remains on the earth. Demons are angels that rebelled against God and fell with Satan." The more you feed these spirits and demons the more they grow based on what you feed them. These spirits want to exist, so they are attracted to people that have something in common with the vices they had when they were in the earth realm.

Solace interrupted, "This sounds different than generational curses."

"Yes, it is slightly different," Love responded. The situation with the young lady is about spirits that have attached themselves to her. These are familiar spirits. The spirits are familiar with the sins she has welcomed into her life. There may be generational curses with her too, but she did not tell me enough. Did you pick up anything from her?"Love asked.

"No nothing at all," Solace confirmed.

"It is very important to be careful with these spirits and demons because they are looking for hosts," Love warned.

Solace asked, "Generational curses are habits or behaviors that are passed down through the family, right?"

"Yes!" Love responded. He continued. "Every person has spiritual information that passes through the bloodline. In the past, people spoke more about spirits. People would make this connection with spirits because they were more receptive. In today's world, people hardly speak to each other anymore. As humans become more and more disconnected spiritual information is being lost. In the past elders and families knew their neighbors and kingdoms and passed on a family's history and spiritual history. Information was kept through stories, rituals, and nature. African Americans in particular, lost a tremendous amount of spiritual information due to the slave trade. For example, A family in the past knew about another family's history and was able to advise if it was wise to marry or not. In some cases, even arranged a marriage. Elders would advise if two people were equally yoked. It wasn't just yoked financially but yoked spiritually. If a family had a history of abuse, sexual immorality, or dishonesty, and they were not compatible with your spirit, the elders would offer advice, and in some cases intervene.

Spirits carry all of the things that are unseen to the human eye such as courage, fear, and energy, in the way that cells carry blood to the heart to have a physical existence.

All of us have light and darkness inside. All of us have angels and demons assigned to us. We as people never know what demons are waiting inside. When the inside meets the outside, we never know what's going to happen. For example, addiction, some people can drink alcohol and are fine but when certain people drink alcohol, they develop an addiction. We call it a chemical reaction or bad luck. I want you to know that it is also spiritual. Other people are able to beat impossible addictions even if it is too heavy narcotics when the light *inside* is greater than the demons that are waiting inside. Some people are unable to *beat* addiction, so the demons that were waiting inside overpower the outside force that was put into the body.

Another example is soul ties. What happens when another person, soul, or spirit gets inside of you? Is it by coincidence that we are more inclined toward certain people? We find ourselves more comfortable with, connected to, trusting of, and loving to specific people. Why? In this same way, people become sexually or emotionally connected to another person. What happens when a person has spiritual baggage you are unaware of? What if strong spirits follow them or their flesh? Each person is made of flesh and spirit even when the physical body dies the spirit becomes something else.

People can connect with some people and even though spirits are released their spiritual ties and bonds are <u>not</u> strong. People with spiritual familiarity should **not** be linked because the history and the connections are too strong. And just like alcohol or drugs, when that spiritual familiarity or history is put inside of another person, we don't know how it will interact with the demons inside. Now, this being said, when certain people get together disaster will always be the result. The bible says, do not be unequally yoked. But some people do not know their spiritual history or the ties that bind them. The most deadly ties are the ones that cannot be seen or the ones that people don't know exist. Our friend Sky that came in today is soul tied.

"This is very troubling to me," Solace said with sadness.

"Why?" Love asked.

Solace explained, "Well, because a person is going along in life, and they may meet someone and simply may be looking for love and because of spiritual things they can get trapped inside of another person. How does a person break a soul tie?" Solace asked.

Love attempted to explain. "It is different for everyone, but it starts with being honest. Sometimes they don't want to get away from someone that is not good for them. A person must ask their inner person questions like, do you hold value to yourself? A person has to have great self-awareness to even ask these questions."

"How does a person break a soul tie?" Solace asked again.

Love attempted to explain again, "I don't have all the answers but unequivocally prayer and fasting. What one needs to break is inside of each and every one of us. A person knows all the details as to why they are attached to a certain person. In order to break a soul tie, you need assistance from God. A soul is something you cannot see. Confess, pray, and decide to walk away. Most importantly, a soul tie is broken when the need to love yourself is greater than the love for the other person."

Solace shook her head and said, "Wow! People have it hard."

Love established, "I cannot help this young woman. She is not my assignment. I'll never get past the surface.

"I'll help her if she wants to be helped," Solace confirmed.

## 5

### The Revealed Belongs to Us!

Dr. Abishai Malcam was a man of perfect order. In his bedroom, he had two nightstands, 12 shirts, 12 pairs of pants, 10 suits, six pairs of shoes, 14 boxers, 14 undershirts, one pair of sneakers, three pairs of shoes, six plates, and six glasses. In his immaculate home, the books had to be returned as soon as they were read. Spills had to be wiped immediately. Laundry had to be washed every three days, nails clipped, and it was important to do things in the same motions and rhythm. He was born with a different name that was changed Dr. Abishai Malcam had six hundred and twenty-three tiny slices that ran from the top of his neck all the way down his spine. The only time the slices could be seen was at Binka!

The drums had already started when he entered.

"Whoa, whoa! ..............Whoa!" the people sang.

"Whoa, whoa,.....Whoa, whoa!"

"Da dum , da dum dum, da dum ,da dum dum, da da da dum dum,  da da da dum dum, da dum dum."

The people swayed. The congregation wore red to attract the attention of the spirits. As they allowed one foot to hit the middle of the circle and then the other, sweat had already formed on their heads and they were full of joy. Some people wore smiles, and others cried, as they allowed the spirits to enter in and out of their bodies. They danced, some kneeled, and some shook. Dr. Abashai Malcam began the dance that ushered him into trance mode. The women brought him the flame. The congregation recited together.

"The secret things belong to the LORD, but the things **revealed** belong to us and to our children forever!" They repeated it a little louder. "The secret things belong to the Lord, but the things revealed belong to our children forever." They got even louder, "The secret things belong to the Lord, but the things revealed belong to our children forever." They all clapped twice and quietly rolled over the crowd.

Dr. Abishai Malcam began, "knowledge will transcend us! Deuteronomy 29:29 is the scripture that we stand on to gain entry into knowledge." He looked over the crowd from left to right and saw faces holding sweat and chests going up and down from the entry ceremony.

He continued, "There was a disagreement long ago. There were some who chose one side because they believed one god was over another. The truth is they were equal gods. That is why one cannot eradicate the other. The people cried out and they believed day after day that there will be justice for the god they served who will come out of the sky and lock up the devil. These people do not know the whole story. Even though something inside of themselves tells them something is missing they don't even believe their own intuition. Jesus himself said that you and I are capable of doing the same things that he was able to do but his own people don't believe it! Jesus said, "Whoever believes in me will also do the works that I do; and greater works than these will he do, because I am going to the Father" (John 14:12). We believe in Jesus, but we know more!"

"Yayee!!" A woman in the congregation screamed in agreement.

"There is a hierarchy on both sides. The father, the son, the Holy Spirit, and angels. What of our hierarchy? What happened to the missing scriptures? A demon is underneath the devil. These things are spiritual things. How do spirits manifest themselves on earth? Through gods! Gods are the acknowledgment of humans that the spiritual world exists.  A god has to be acknowledged on earth by us in order to exist in the physical plane. What do gods need? BLOOD! The blood is the door between the spiritual and the physical world.  How do gods get blood? Gods get blood from demons and spirits. What are spirits? Those that have been on earth in the physical realm before! The more blood you feed the spirits, the spirits feed the gods on earth and humans acknowledge the god and the portal stays open. When demons extract blood from living things, they keep the portals open. The best way to extract blood from humans is to allow them to indulge in the vices of their choice that they already like to do." The audience clapped and nodded their heads in agreement. "We believe in Jesus because Jesus is God, spirit, blood, and human. He taught us that we can reincarnate. There were other people on earth such as the Egyptians who believed that man could come back after death. The knowledge disappeared. Or did it?"

"No sir!" yelled a man in the back.

"It is important for us to understand the importance of order and repetition. This is how we detect imperfections in others. Daily motions and rituals that others may deem senseless motions and rhythms are not useless. They write off their phone combinations and passwords as erratic patterns, but these behaviors are keys to us. These movements are entryways into the spiritual information of others. These motions and habits and addictions and vices help us feed our spirits. People make symbols every day that they deemed senseless motions such as punching passcodes into their phones. You do not have to waste time drawing circles on the floor or long ceremonious incantations if you know a person's blood weakness.

Wait, watch, observe. You can pull spiritual information out of the air. If you know a person's vice and weakness, their blood will follow and you can use it to feed the spirits.  Alcoholics, drug addicts, gamblers, sex addicts, rapists, thieves, cheaters, people addicted to stress and drama, you need those people. Try to fine-tune your antenna to these people and things that are not easy to detect with the eye.

I honor all of you tonight. All of you are special and you have proven yourselves worthy in knowledge; students of observation and devoted in blood. All of you that stand before me have made great sacrifices and our spirits are pleased. The gods are pleased."

Abishai stepped down from the podium and approached the altar. On the altar lay the chunk of wood and the knife. The congregation of fifty lined up and began exposing their vertebrae. Some of the chosen had five slices, some ten, some thirty, or seventy-seven.  As they approached, Abishai lifted the sharp razor and sliced a very deep but thin incision on the surface of their spine. The people started to bleed and sat in the blood chairs designed to allow the blood to flow into a basin. Abishai watched as they freely dripped their blood into the basins. After each person was dripped, he or she was stitched. The stitched members were tired and were given the glass pipe to smoke. The entire process took many hours.

After everyone was bled. The blood was poured on the altar, and the drums started again. The members that were at rest popped up as if they were energized. The blood began to burn.

"The spirits have accepted our offering and our god is pleased. Make your requests known," Abishai announced.

The room erupted in celebration. People threw gold, fruit, and strips of cloth on the altar. They took turns kneeling before the piece of wood that was oddly misshapen, polished, and burned in some places. Some danced, some cried, and others just stared. As they left on their own accord, Abishai gave them each a piece of red thread.

When everyone departed Abishai gathered the remaining blood he collected and prepared to offer it to the spirits. The dark red blood reminded him of the crimson on his mother's blood stained dress when he was a boy. He remembered how he became the man he is now. It started with the murder of his father. The lynching to be exact. Abishai was eight years old when they came at night for his father Eakkon. His mother Loiuse was beaten and raped by the white mob. Then his father was beaten and raped by the white mob. Abishai hid under the bed and could hear the brutality but could not see it. They dragged his father out of their house to the tree in front.

His mother's cries for mercy were met with angry kicks and slaps until no more words were able to come out of her mouth. Eakkon was hoisted up into the tree and released and then silenced as his body swung. After the mob departed Louise did not wait for the body to be removed from the tree. She did not wait for the family to come over to lament and offer prayers. She walked into the house and called Abishai from under the bed. She grabbed his little hand and they started walking through the darkness with no fear left in her body. She would not allow Abishai to see his father hanging from the tree. They walked into the woods of South Carolina. deeper and deeper until the night started to turn into daylight and they kept walking until they saw the small cabin. Abishai remembered the kids at school talking about this cabin where the Hoodoo woman lived that practiced Binka but he thought it was just a story. Abishai's mama Louise started to cry as they reached the doorstep and looked at him for the first time in hours. The small old woman opened the door as if she was waiting for them. Her face was small and pleasant. When she turned around her arms and the part of her back that was visible was covered with old healed whip marks.

"Hi," his mother greeted the woman.

"It's been a long time Louise." The Hoodoo woman replied.

"I need your help grandma Mildred." His mother pleaded.

"*Grandma*?" Abishai thought to himself.

"Nobody comes through that forest unless they need help,"Mildred confirmed.

"They lynched Eakkon." Loiuse revealed.

Abishai thought they killed him but was not sure until he heard his mother tell Ms. Mildred.

Mildred stared at Louise until Louise broke the silence. "Grandma, I said they killed Eakkon."

"I heard you." Mildred replied.  "So, what do you want me to do to them?" She asked.

"I don't want you to hurt them. I want you to protect Abishai." Louise presented humbly.

Mildred stared at her again and asked. "Why don't you do the spell yourself? You know how to do it."

"I got saved and baptized at church. I no longer possess those abilities." Louise confessed.

Mildred sucked her teeth and stared at her again with a mixture of anger and disappointment in her eyes.

"Well, here you are back at Binka." Mildred said sarcastically.

"You know protection would require a blood sacrifice." Mildred reminded Louise.

"This whole land around us is soaked with Black folk blood." His mother Louise said. "His father was lynched a few hours ago and the blood was already paid it's already in the ground."

"Well then, since he is my grandson there is something else. I have something better." Mildred confided.

"What?" His mother asked.

Mildred walked over to the corner of her room and pulled out a brown rag and walked back over to the two of them.

"This here is from Africa." She said and presented and unwrapped the contents to reveal teeth, hair, and finger bones.

"This man here is a Binder Shifter. If Abisahi agrees willingly to allow the Binder to occupy his body and consume his spirit he will be protected and become powerful and all of his knowledge will become Abishai's. Abishai will not only be safe but unstoppable." Mildred promised.

"How does this work?" Louise asked.

"The death ceremony" His grandmother said seriously. "The boy has to be able to agree first."

Abishai was set to the task of fetching water from the well and bringing it back to fill the copper tub. It took him all afternoon to fill the tub. The day turned into afternoon and his grandmother Mildred prepared food for Abishai and his mother. After they ate, his mother slept. Mildred continued to prepare things in the kitchen and chanted. She rocked back and forth a lot and did not say anything to him.

When it became night Mildred started a fire in the yard. She fed him and his mother.

His mother began to ask him questions.

"Abishai, were you afraid when those men came for your daddy?"Louise asked.

"Yes," he answered his mother Louise.

"Do you want to be safe?" His mother asked.

"Yes," He said emphatically.

"Do you want your mother to be safe?" his grandmother Mildred asked.

"Yes" he responded with curiosity in his tone.

"If you want to be safe then you have to tell the spirits that you want them to play with you." Louise compelled.

"Ok" Abishai agreed.

"But not only play with you, you have to let the spirit into your heart." His mother stressed.

"How I do that?" Abishai aked.

"All you have to do is say yes." His mother reassured.

"We will help you," Mildred interjected.

"All you have to do is tell this man he can come in." His mother said as she presented the finger bones to Abishai.

The bones scared Abishai a little.

"Ok, he can come in." Abishai said with no hesitation.

His grandmother Mildred threw some of the finger bones on the fire and the other bones in the copper tub.

"Ok, get in the tub." His mother commanded.

Abishai had never seen a copper tub before and was excited to get in.

The water was warm and the light from the fire shined on his mother and his grandmother's face.

The woman chanted and then they pushed him under. His mother held his head and shoulders down and his grandmother Mildred held his feet. He tried to struggle until he could no longer struggle. He drowned. After he drowned they pulled him out of the tub and Mildred breathed air into his lungs and pushed on his heart. She chanted until he coughed up water and came back to life. His mother rejoiced.

"Is that you Malcam?" Mildred asked the body.

"Yes, it is us,'' Malcam responded from Abishai's body.

"Please, from now on I will be called Abishai Malcam." He stated.

Louise began to cry.

"This is what you wanted. You wanted to save your son and he will be saved and more." Mildred confirmed.

"I know but he is no longer a child." Louise dismayed.

"Well, you can leave him here with us now," Mildred insisted.

The next day Louise departed the forest without her son.

## 6

## Young and Beautiful

Marlon sat in the back of the restaurant and watched Sky walk in as other men acknowledged her beauty by staring. As she passed them to walk toward him, he enjoyed the envious eyes that followed her to their table.  Sky took off her coat to reveal a flawless figure draped in a cobalt blue dress.  Marlon felt pride in her arrival, kissed her on both cheeks, and pulled out her chair. Before he even had a chance to sit down, she belted out,

"You have an interview with Senator Smith!"

"What?" Marlon asked in confusion.

Sky elaborated. "I got you an interview with the Senator.  I think he's going to run for President, and you will be the first with an exclusive interview." Marlon smiled.

"Don't smile at me! You're paying for lunch and I'm ordering everything."  Sky joked.

Marlon's face changed from a smile to concern. He asked. "I know you are trying to keep it light. Are we just going to ignore the elephant in the room? What's going on with the Maker's House? I've been calling you. How are you?"

Sky acknowledged, "Yes, I know I'm just trying to catch my breath. My heart is heavy. I am going through a lot right now." Marlon ordered a bottle of wine and shots for them. He knew they would be there for hours discussing everything that came to mind. Sky always came bearing gifts and today was especially good. She placed the flight confirmation and hotel reservations on the table along with his media pass as she tried to ignore the situation.

"I truly appreciate this but I want to hear about you right now and how I can help," Marlon reassured.

"You're already helping by being here." Sky replied. Marlon reached for Sky's hands and kissed them. He meditated on how comfortable Sky was with him now and how many years it had taken them to get back to that point.

"So what's happening with you?"Marlon asked again.

Sky responded, "I am so mad that Preston died and I think about him all the time. I'm worried about the kids and what's going to happen to all of them."

"Wow Skit, I know this is a lot to think about"

"Remember what happened in Rome?" Marlon's smile slowly faded and the intensity in his eyes increased. He could not remember Rome without remembering it all. Remember was a deadly word in their relationship. He let out a deep breath and said, Yes. " I remember."

Marlon's mind wandered to their past. The memory was like eating something delicious and biting the tongue at the same time. Sky excused herself to go to the bathroom and Marlon was already taking a trip down their memory lane. In college Sky's reputation on campus preceded her. Her intelligence and drive, only surpassed by

Her devotion to Kern Grant, were legendary, and her beauty, intelligence, and ambition were only accessories to compliment his career. The other men often talked about their failed attempts to date Sky and her proper upright manner. Some of them found pleasure in the fact that Kern was rotating Sky in an endless bowl of women.  Sky knew Kern's type. She heard whispers and rumors around campus that he was a good-looking, forceful, rapist. Sky set a trail of breadcrumbs to her door. Kern was respectful towards Sky in the beginning and gentle until his true nature kicked in. She knew it was only a matter of time.

Kern's sickness demanded that he had to be in control and take it, and when he came to rape her.  Sky made it easy. She resisted just enough for him to get his feeling of control but the next day she made him look good in public; showing up by his side with compliments on her lips looking polished and refined.  She intoxicated Kern, and he was disgusted with himself, but this woman knew how to medicate him. Kern Grant was the son of the Governor, and his family was deeply rooted in one of Boston's fastest-growing churches. Her attendance at church and political gatherings enabled her to make connections. She tolerated his indiscretions and sickness in exchange for being a part of his world. When he broke up with Sky, his family and friends were shocked because she made him look good. Sky showed no signs of being wounded. She could be spotted on campus attending activities and hosting debates. She maintained business as usual. Marlon heard about the breakup just like everyone else but also wondered what the real story was. He grew up near Kern and knew about the rapes, DUI's, and charges that the Grant family paid to cover up.

Marlon was the Teacher's Assistant for Sky's Advanced Constitutional law and advanced legal writing class. Marlon held his breath as he read Sky's paper about children in foster homes with parents who have a mental illnesses. After class, Marlon handed Sky her paper and said, "Your paper moved me, and your research was very thorough and compelling. I was wondering if you would be one of four people that we use to discuss your topic, research, and writing style."

"I am not the right person for this kind of assignment. I think you should choose someone else." Sky told him with a dismissive tone.

"Why are you not the right person?" Marlon persisted. Sky recognized Marlon not only as the class TA, but he was also in attendance at many social events she attended. He also held her attention because she knew he knew Kern and saw him in a picture with his family.

"There is nothing more important to me than my career and I do not have time to do things that do not contribute to that goal." Sky said sternly.

Marlon tried to persuade her, "I see, so the children that you talk about in your research and the broken system that you describe and the solutions that you came up with are a politician's dream. If you were to implement some of the solutions you offer in your paper based on the research you presented, I do not understand how this is not connected to your career. This is your career. The beauty of it is that it's all based on you and what you will build and put together." Sky stared at Marlon and smiled. It was like someone saw her for the first time in her life. They started walking and talking and that day turned into another meeting after class and another and then, every other day, and then every day.

The connection was so organic, easy, and sometimes chaotic. Fall turned to winter, winter to spring, and spring approached summer. Sky and Marlon were with each other every day.  They conversed about everything under the sun. They argued loud and fiercely about politics and the role of women and men. They explored every corner of the city and ate at every restaurant they could afford. They watched every movie that came out together and reviewed every album. Marlon shared every poem and essay he had ever written with Sky and Sky listened. They spent late nights studying at the library and drinking coffee and they stayed awake for days. But It was the conversations they had in the dark holding each other's hands that meant the most and sealed their friendship. Sky was the first person Marlon ever told about his mother and father being unhappy in their marriage. and how he always felt alone. Marlon was the first person Sky ever told about her mother's mental illness and the multiple rapes and beatings that happened to her when she was in foster care.  They built a sanctuary and fortified it by giving each other all the hugs they never received as children.  They had secret laughs, signals, and for the first time, they could be kids.  One night Sky said to Marlon, "I won a spot to do the political internship in Rome this summer."

 "You are broke, no money, NADA!! How are you supposed to go to another country?!"Marlon responded.

"I don't know but, this is an opportunity of a lifetime. I've always wanted to go." Sky said enthusiastically.

Those words sparked something in Marlon and there was nothing more that he wanted than to spend the summer with Sky in Italy. Marlon applied for a teacher's position.

Marlon rushed to tell her the great news of being offered the teacher's position abroad. He wanted to let her know she wouldn't have to worry about paying rent for traveling for the summer, and that she could stay with him and study abroad. Sky couldn't believe Marlon did this for her. Nobody had ever done anything like this for her before. She could not wait to see Rome.

Studying in Rome was glorious. The experience was a dream actualized. Their small apartment was old, beautiful and filled with ancient character. Rome was special in that way. A person could walk down the street and run into something that was made thousands of years before. The Colosseum, Palatine Hill, The Vatican, The Pantheon, Trevi Fountain, the Spanish steps were the perfect romantic setting for lovers. The ancient city inspired their scholarship as they excelled as students. They studied and took the train to other nearby European countries. They felt alive and safe and their memories were decorated with each other. All of their senses were ignited, engaged and they fought, laughed, ate the most amazing food and happiness was the soundtrack to their time in Rome.

On the night of the incident. They checked into the hotel across from the Villa Borghese. They had to stay one more night before going to Sardinia. The wind blew the flaps on the outside of the large old-fashioned window. Sky awakened at 3:33 a.m. She wasn't sure about the circle which seemed like a shadow on the floor. The moon was so bright in the sky she couldn't comprehend what she was seeing. The circle moved closer to the floor. And she saw a man's back as clear as day surrounded by spirits. He knelt to the spirits, and she witnessed a deal of some kind was being made. He cut himself with tiny slits, one of the male spirits whispered in his ear, and he turned his head to the right, careful not to turn all the way around to face her. It was clear he was aware of her presence. The spirit began to approach Sky, coming closer to the puddle. Then the puddle raised itself off the ground into the air and as the spirit came closer. Sky grabbed it and tried to pull, unsure if this was really happening. It squealed in fear and Sky realized it was not afraid of her but afraid of something behind her in the room she was in. As she put her hand into the puddle, it felt unbearable cold. Then, suddenly she caught on fire. Sky started to scream and she awakened Marlon.  She stripped and ran out of the apartment with no clothes on, convinced she was on fire. Marlon chased her into the park and tried to convince her that she was not on fire. She peeled and scratched her own skin and screamed for help.  A group tried to help calm Sky and Marlon tried to cover her nakedness. Sky fought them all and then just as suddenly as she caught on fire she realized she was not on fire. Sky was embarrassed to be naked outside. Marlon quickly brought her inside. They stayed awake that night Marlon rocking her in his arms. They checked out the next morning as people whispered about the night before. They headed for the coast. On the way to the coast, Sky told Marlon about the spirits her mother used to fear, her visions, and what she experienced the night before. He did not know what to say but he believed her. When they arrived at their apartment rental on the coast they were both exhausted and fell into a deep sleep.


Marlon woke up in a dark room lit by the moon. He saw Sky standing on the balcony staring at the ocean. The heat of the room quickly consumed him, and he realized the hot sticky summer air was getting to him too. He got out of bed quietly and easily because he didn't want to scare her as he walked toward the balcony. Sky felt his presence behind her and reached for his hand. He instinctively put his hand in hers. She started walking down the stairs and he followed her into the sand. She walked faster and so did he. She started jogging and so did he. Then she started running and they both hit the water and screamed. The night was hot, but the cold ocean water was more than they bargained for. Sky laughed and screamed, "Why didn't you stop me?"

Marlon laughed as the water hit waist level. Sky's fear kicked in and she realized it was dangerous and that some shark might eat them alive. She jumped on Marlon's back with the fear of a child.

"Please get me out of here!" She commanded.

Marlon teased, "Oh my God, Why did you run into the water? Now you're begging for mercy?" Marlon laughed so hard he could not collect himself. He was fighting the tide and his laughter. Sky was crying and laughing at the same time.

"Please get me outta here!" She begged.

Marlon said, "Repeat after me…I…Sky Jones."

"I…Sky Jones," she repeated.

"Promise today." Marlon instructed.

"Promise today." Sky repeated

"That Marlon is my hero,"Marlon insisted.

"I'm not saying that!" Sky replied.

"Well, I'm gonna leave you here in the ocean," Marlon assured.

Feeling her heart rate increasing, Sky repeated, "Marlon is my hero."

"And from this day forward,"Marlon continued.

"And from this day forward, Sky repeated.

"I'm devoted to him." Marlon concluded.

Sky hesitated as Marlon walked deeper into the ocean.

"Woman, I will leave you right here with the sharks and the sharp rocks." Sky screamed and repeated Marlon's sentence. She concluded. "I'm devoted to him."

She held him tight as he gave her a piggyback ride to shore.

She laughed as Marlon jokingly yelled at her, "Stay still so I won't fall! Sky's shivering body and lips on his earlobes made the temperature in his body rise.  Sky could feel the muscles in Marlon's back and legs as he carried her to the house.

They reached the bottom of the stairs and Sky slowly slid off Marlon's back.

"Thank you. I needed that," she said.

"Me too," Marlon replied.

When Sky reached the top of the steps, she sat down on the patio furniture and started ringing out the bottom of her dress. Marlon placed her feet in his lap and brushed the sand off her feet and legs. His movements evolved into slow methodical movements. He stood and extended his hand.

Sky put her hand in his hand and felt her ears tingle inside as she followed him into the moonlit room. The heat in the room made taking their clothes off seem natural and easy. He unbuttoned her top three buttons and kissed her slowly. Sky was aware of her nipples flaring as her wet dress passed over her head. Marlon backed up towards the bed as they kissed. The sheets on the bed were warm on Sky's back and Marlon's tongue was even hotter than the temperature of that night of the heatwave.

Marlon remembered everything from the night, but images flashed through his mind like he was watching a movie. The memory was slow motion in some parts and fast forward in others. Sky's lips, the temperature of the room, the speed of the rhythm, he especially remembered her touching his lips and her telling him, "I love you!"

They fell asleep and woke up in the morning together. He loved the texture of her skin and how her hair was out of place in the morning. She looked at him the next day and she was not in a rush to leave his side. They spent the next week on the coast before they would leave Italy and return home.

At home, in the States, it was even better than Italy itself. They enjoyed long walks at night, slow dancing in the apartment, making love, and laying together all day. Marlon never did forget the day Sky chose Kern over him.

Kern's mother arrived at Sky's apartment to her surprise. Sky reluctantly opened the door. Her heart was beating so fast. Bernadette Grant was the Governor's wife and made Sky nervous. She strolled through the apartment into any room she pleased as if she were looking for someone. Finally, she made herself comfortable on the couch. Bernadette started, "My son is not very intelligent when it comes to making the right decisions and choosing people that can propel his career. Sky, he needs a woman like you who knows what she wants and how to get it. We all have a mutual interest in mind. This woman is accusing my son of forcing her to have sex with him. We want you to marry him and stand by him and maybe even testify for him at the trial."

"I don't know if I can do that." Sky said as she looked at Mrs. Grant with a confirmation glance that said she knew Kern was guilty. Mrs. Grant interrupted her stare.

Bernadette admitted, "We both know my son has a strange pallet but most women know how he is already. He is handsome and wealthy, and they choose to put themselves in harm's way."

Sky was uncomfortable with the conversation and blurted out, "I'm pregnant!"

Mrs. Grant smiled slowly. "Even better! Does the baby belong to my son?"

"No, Mrs. Grant." Sky disclosed.

"How far along are you?" Bernadette asked.

"I'm ten weeks," Sky confirmed.

"Well, you and my son broke up around that time give or take a couple of months. This is not a problem. In college we all take lovers and it is easy for a woman to get confused about the timing of events. The baby could be my son's. What jury would convict a husband and a father? You stay with my son and marry him. As a member of our family, all of your dreams would come true. We would certainly take care of you and I couldn't possibly have my grandchild without a name." Bernadette said with absolute certainty.

"My baby already has a father and I love him very much," Sky assured.

"Does he know you're pregnant?" Bernadette asked.

"He does not know I'm pregnant yet." Sky confided.

Bernadette moved in close to Sky and lowered her voice down to a  whisper. "When I first met you, I knew you were a woman on the rise. I liked you immediately. As far as I'm concerned, the baby is my son's.  Our name attached to yours can fast-track your career. The life a person wants is based on a series of choices. You are faced with the choice of love or power. There are not many women that would allow a man his imperfections and indiscretions and then show up beside him the next day.

He owes you! We owe you. Why go through the whole process and not finish well? You have already proven yourself and put in the work. Now it is time for you to collect and we are offering you the life you have been working so hard for."

"I need time to think about it." Sky heard herself say.

"All I need is a yes." Bernadette insisted.

Mrs. Grant left the black box on the coffee table and left the apartment. Sky opened the box when she left and inside was a beautiful marquise cut engagement ring and realized she was holding her future in her hands.

Marlon arrived at Sky's apartment as if he won the lottery and didn't notice her sad disposition at all. He started speaking right away, "Come with me!" he said.

"What?" Sky questioned.

"Come with me?" He commanded in a playful tone.

"Come where?" Sky asked.

Marlon tugged at her sweater and said, "come to the Kitchen." Sky followed as he logged into his computer and opened the letter.

Marlon continued, "I was offered a full-time position in Italy. They are going to pay for the apartment and give us money to relocate."

"Wow! That's great!" Sky managed to say. A million things ran through her mind. She saw the jubilation in his spirit, the smile on his face, and an opportunity of a lifetime was at his feet, but she did not want to move to

Italy right now. Sky needed to finish law school, and she couldn't tell him about the baby. Sky felt saliva flood her mouth and her throat was blocked. She had not felt that way since she was abandoned as a child. She concealed the fact that she was open, vulnerable, and angry.

She was mad at herself for allowing this feeling. The laughs and this level of devotion opened her. She was reminded of the promise she made to herself. *Become powerful and stop being powerless.* The only thing she could do was match his bad news with fake excitement. "I have great news too! Kern came over today and asked me to marry him. Marlon felt like another person walked through him and looked at the goosebumps on his arm.

"And?" Marlon asked as His nostrils flared.

"And I said yes." Sky said as her whole body felt weak.

Marlon squinted his eyes in confusion. Anger filled his body and he said, "You said, yes!?" He sat down at the kitchen table. "You're joking! What the fuck do you mean you said yes?" He asked and stood on his feet. "What have we been doing here?" He covered his face with his hands and paced back and forth. "Wow! I'm shocked that you said yes," he said sternly.

"I still have feelings for him." Sky insisted.

"Do you still have feelings for him? Marlon questioned. "Fuck that! I know you Sky, you don't love him. You just want to climb to the top of the food chain" Marlon condemned. "Don't do this, please!" he pleaded.

Sky questioned, "It's not like we were going to get married right? You're talking about leaving"

"I wasn't planning on marrying you right now, but it was in our future." Marlon clarified. "I can't compete with a marriage proposal RIGHT NOW. What the fuck are you talking about Sky? Who are you?" Marlon questioned.

Marlon moved closer and eliminated the air and space between them and he looked her in the eyes.

"Do you love him?" He demanded.

"He gives me what I need." Sky said as she thought about what Bernadette said.

"Then I'm happy for you." Marlon mocked.

Sky leaned in for a quick fake hug, but Marlon pulled her into his body. "DO YOU LOVE ME!" He asked. He held her by the waist and back, increasing his grip and inhaling her smell until she felt all his strength around her.

He squeezed her because he did not want to let her go, he squeezed her because he could not bear to ask her what she needed, and he squeezed her to ease the devastation and the impact on his heart of what she told him. He pulled her into his body so close they stood belly to belly, so close to the baby that he knew nothing about, and she felt his heart beating fast and his breath on the side of her face.

She hugged him back like she was seeing her mother again like he was with her every time she cried herself to sleep as a child-like she was swallowing needles. He squeezed her so hard she knew he would squeeze the tears out of her eyes. So, she let go and he let go. Well, it seems like we both have something to celebrate.   Marlon left the apartment and Sky thought she was going to drown to death in her own tears.  A few hours later she called Mrs. Grant.

"Mrs. Grant, my answer is yes." Sky said with sorrow in her heart.

"Great! I'll tell my son the two of you are getting married. Well, you have made a great choice." Mrs. Grant confirmed.

When Sky returned from the restroom this is what Marlon remembered.  He was also reminded this is why Sky always came bearing gifts.  She walked back to their table with two shots of Marlon's favorite Bourbon.  He smiled and drank both shots and also had to remember that he forgave Sky.  She placed her hand on his thigh and his heart softened.

"So what were you saying before you went to the bathroom?" He asked.

"I was saying, remember what happened in Rome when I thought I was on fire?" She asked.

"Yes, I remember." He validated.

"I am starting to see things like that again." She admitted.

Marlon blew the breath out of his mouth and rubbed the back of his neck. "I'm worried about you Skit. Did you tell Dr. Davis?"He asked.

"I told her but I didn't tell her, tell her, everything because I don't want her to think I'm crazy.  I know the stuff I'm seeing and feeling is real." Sky confided.

"Well then, Why not tell her everything?" Marlon asked compassionately. Sky moved in closer and lowered her voice.

"Marlon, you know how this goes. Therapists are mandated to report certain things. If your experience does not fit into one of those boxes then a person could lose everything. Especially with everything that happened at the Maker's House. I would be judged if someone found out." Sky admitted.

"I totally understand." Marlon agreed.

"So what is your plan?" he asked.

"Sharon took me to these people. She said they could help me but I was creeped out by the old man." Sky explained.

"Why?" he asked.

Sky expressed her concern, "He was asking personal questions and I am a private person. I thought he was just another person trying to make money."

"I don't think Sharon would take you anywhere bad. She loves you. Sometimes conventional help is not the only answer.  Sometimes you need someone that can help you off the record." Marlon suggested.

Sky thought about what Marlon said, "Maybe you're right"

I'm always right!" Marlon said sarcastically. "Now let's order dinner. I'm starving!"

Sky was relieved to be here with Marlon. "Ok, let's eat," She agreed.

7

<u>When Fly Girls Get Old</u>

The men and women standing around Dudley looked like flies landing on old dry feces and failed to see that the universe around them was changing. The universities purchased and started rebuilding the torn down old structures and replacing them. There were signs that read, *Coming Soon New Dudley Station*. There was a huge picture hanging in the station that gave a preview of what the finished construction would look like in the future. The picture did not depict any people of color, only plans of pristine streets and high-rise buildings.

Jackie was the only woman standing with a group of old men. The group did not know Dudley Station was no longer a place to hang. A pain hit Jackie as Paris passed her and did not acknowledge her at all. Jackie was glad that her senses were altered by her earlier consumption of alcohol because the silence would have devastated her. Paris did not blink as she passed her mother at Dudley Station. The two women caught eyes, and it was like looking in a mirror. Neither of the women blinked but the silence was loud, and it screamed. 'I know everything about you, and I know it well,' Paris dared her to speak. Jackie would not dare. Jackie forfeited her right as a mother years ago and was only an old fly girl now. She was surprised her mother was still alive looking as horrid as ever. Paris started to breathe slowly and shallowly, her technique to hold back emotions.

She knew the commute home was going to be unbearable. As she looked out of the window of the bus the community outside passed by. Paris was overwhelmed with a shower of bad memories from the past, and she prepared herself to become mentally ill. She vividly remembered the broken pieces from her childhood that made her want to throw up in her own mouth. She fought the brutal memories that were coming to her mind. She turned up the music on her phone as loud as they would go. Paris tried to watch the people instead of being in her own head. Her techniques did not work.  She searched through her bag for the pills Dr. Malcam gave her, but she left them at home on that day of all days. She tried the tapping technique he had taught her to release the energy. The methods were useless, for her mother was too big of a trigger. She remembered.

Her room was the coldest room in the house located in the back. Jackie sold their furniture to sponsor a coke and weed party. Paris was so angry she left and went to stay at Grandma Jessie's house for weeks. She eventually had to go home to get more clothes.

Paris heard a loud slam and turned around. Kenny, her mother's boyfriend yelled, "You think nobody would notice your stupid ass being gone for two weeks? Just because your Mama don't respect me don't mean your little stank ass wont. I'll kick your ass. Your mama don't even know how to raise you. You know you have rules." Paris was so scared. He was big and towered over her. He weighed about three hundred pounds and looked like he never washed up. He had bumps all over his face. Her fears left and she remembered that she hated him.

"You ain't my father!" Paris reminded him.

"Where is your father?" He asked. "You're right. I ain't your father"

He then grabbed for her, but she moved out of the way, grabbed one of the ashtrays off the dresser, and hit him in the head as hard as she could. He fell against the wall, and she knew he was going to hit her, so she ran to the door. She purposely knocked things over as she ran by them to make noise and slow him down.

"Ma!" Paris screamed as she ran by her mother's room. She made it all the way to the living room and felt her hand being crushed on the locks. He grabbed her hair and dragged her across the rug from the living room to the kitchen. "Ma!" Paris yelled again. Paris scratched his face and bit him, but he did not release his grip. He grabbed her by the neck and punched her in the stomach so hard it shocked her. Her face was burning from the slap that came next. "My arms hurt," she yelled.

Kenny whispered. "You're just like your mother. You'll never be good for nothing except a good fuck." He took her and threw her on the floor and pinned her hands down the kitchen floor. He put all his weight on her and gave her a creepy smile. He had beaten her before but this time she knew that this was not the same. Paris was exhausted. She started crying.

"My mother's gonna kill you! Mother fucker! Ma! Ma!" Paris screamed for Jackie.

Kenny let her scream until her voice was gone.

He whispered, "Your mother's so high right now."

Paris begged, "Please no, no, no, no."

He slid his belt off and jammed it in her mouth.

"Shut up," He told her. as he squeezed her face.

She was wearing her pink hoodie with white jeans. He ripped her jeans down and she tried to hold them up with her hands. She broke her nails trying to keep them up. He punched her in the face again, the blow made black spots appear in her vision, and she was dizzy. She was so tired. He ripped her panties that had the ice cream cones design off her body.

He put his body between her legs. She saw him take his penis out and she panicked and tried to get up again. She had never seen a penis before. He hit her again and then pushed himself into her so hard and angry she thought she would die. It felt like someone hit her with a bat in her private spot. She looked up at the ceiling with leak stains and the table with the empty beer cans and felt the cold floor under her and the pain from the blows.

She smelled the liquor on his breath. His sweat fell on her cheek, and some fell in her eye, and it burned. She could do nothing but lay there and think to herself. *My mother is in her room.* He finished, stood over her, looked down at her breathing heavily, pulled up his pants, and walked out of the house.

Paris lay there and wished her mother would walk in and react. She cried and wanted to disappear. She was shaking and could not believe what he did to her. She wished for so many things at that moment: She wished she hadn't gone home. She wished she had a father to call. She wished she wasn't born. She crawled over to the phone and called Grandma Jessie. Grandma Jessie's voice made Paris swell. She wanted to say something, but she could only cry.

Grandma Jessie asked, "Paris, are you ok?" Paris tried to scream nothing, but dry crackling air came out of her mouth.

Grandma Jessie said, "Baby is that you? Baby, you ok? I'm on my way!"

Paris wanted to yell, "Come get me, come get me, come get me!" Nothing came out. She was only able to gasp for air. It took Miss Jessie about seven minutes to drive to her daughter's house, but it seemed like hours to Paris.

Grandma Jessie walked in to see Paris folded up in the corner. Paris' hair was on the floor and her panties were balled up in her hand. She walked over to her and put her arms around her. Paris never saw her grandmother cry in her whole life, but today slow tears came to Miss Jessie's eyes and rolled down her cheeks. Paris saw Grandma Jessie fill a big bucket on the floor with cold water, march into Jackie's bedroom, and splashed it on her daughter. She slapped her face over and over and over.

"Jackie, you let this man do this to your baby?" Grandma Jessie screamed.

"What?" Jackie answered with slurred speech.

Paris heard her grandmother's fist pound her mother's flesh repeatedly until she was exhausted herself and realized Jackie was so high that her blows didn't matter. Paris stared at the room and could only hear the words and see the shadows on the floor. She stared straight ahead and didn't even notice Pharaoh stood at the front door patiently waiting for Grandma's instructions.

Grandma Jessie came out of the room and put a blanket around Paris. "You ain't never coming back here again!" Grandma Jessie yelled. She instructed Pharaoh to carry Paris to the car. Paris didn't want to be touched but was too weak to protest.

Pharaoh was only sixteen, but he was tall and solid. He lifted Paris up and she could feel pain all over her body. Paris could see that Pharaoh felt sorry for her. He cried as Miss Jessie cried. Miss Jessie was disgusted and upset.

Paris lay in the back seat and stared at the top of the buildings as they drove to her grandma's house. Paris never saw her grandma get mad or cry, but that day her eyes were red, filled with tears, and puffy. Pharaoh drove the car and did not say anything. Pharaoh drove the car into the back of the house, and Pharaoh gently lifted Paris out of the back seat as Grandma led them up the backstairs of the house.

Grandma Jessie did not say anything. She just cried, and Paris watched her work. She ran bathwater and brought Paris into the bathroom. Paris felt strange being naked, but Grandma kept her eyes to the ground and cleaned Paris' sores with peroxide. She took splinters out of her stomach. She kept her eyes to the floor and periodically slapped her hand on the floor or the sink in anger. She helped her into the tub and her scratches stung. She washed the dried blood off her face, and then she walked out of the bathroom. Paris sat in the hot water and cried silent tears. Grandma returned with herbs and said,

"I need you to open your legs for me. Don't be shamed I want to make sure this doesn't turn out bad for you. I'm gonna put this on the outside and I want you to put this on the inside. After Paris put what looked like a tea bag inside, Mamma washed her legs and private parts. Her legs had welt marks going up and down them, and the soap burned. Grandma finished and came back in with the towel. The water was light brown when Grandma Jessie finished. She dried her and put clean sweatpants and a t-shirt on Paris. She brushed her hair and wrapped it.

Pharaoh sat on the porch outside fuming, thinking about Paris. Paris was always kind to him. She was his first friend. They became friends the first day they met at Miss Jessie's house, and she had been his best friend ever since. Her smile was always able to make him smile. She shared everything with him, always made sure he ate, and would leave money on his dresser with a note that would say FOR CHIPS, FOR DRINK, FOR CANDY, FOR SHOES, EVEN FOR WEED. They spent hours watching movies and eating noodles. She was the one that taught him the game of Monster killers. They would confess secrets, write them down, bury them in the ground, throw them in the ocean, or even burn them as they would proclaim, "Monster killers!" and laugh. Paris helped him heal through that game of burying deeper and darker secrets until he feared nothing. These thoughts were drowning him and made him more and more furious when Dr. Abishai Malcam arrived.

"Good evening," the doctor greeted.

"No, It's not good," Pharaoh replied as he escorted the doctor inside. Pharaoh ascended the stairs to alert

Grandma Jessie of the doctor's presence, and then he went back to the porch. The doctor waited inside for Miss Jessie and handed her a package.

On his way out, he told Pharaoh, "You know there is a special awful place for men that do horrible things to children."

"Oh yeah?" Pharaoh was curious.

"Yes," Dr. Malcam confirmed. "I actually have a special place for them."

According to street code, Pharaoh knew that was his cue to take a walk to find out what the good doctor was talking about or to let it fly. Pharaoh stood up and walked, a confirmation of sorts he was interested. Dr. Malcam continued, "If a man like Kenny were to show up at my lab with you, we could ask him what gives him the authority to touch the innocent."

"What's in it for you?" Pharaoh asked.

The doctor removed all expression from his face and told Pharaoh "Well, let's put it like this, you can do with him whatever you want, and it will be none of my business and I will do with him what I will, and it will be none of your business."

Pharaoh was not surprised that the clean-cut doctor was dirty. The doctor's response sent chills through his body.

"I want to keep his teeth!" Pharaoh confirmed.

"Absolutely, I'll see you soon!" Dr. Malcam agreed.

Pharaoh knew exactly who Kenny was. He sold it to him many times. Two days later Pharaoh got his chance. Pharaoh only needed to wait a little while as Kenny was a fiend and soon, he would be looking for another hit. Pharaoh had the best drugs on the street. Kenny came to him to cop as a creature of habit. Kenny nervously approached Pharoah and the other men standing on the corner of Charles Street and Geneva Ave. The other dealers nodded their heads in acknowledgment that Kenny was Pharaoh's fiend.  Pharaoh slowly lured him deeper into the slim alley on Charles Street. Kenny scratched his skin ferociously and couldn't wait to put the needle in his arm. Pharoah watched him crouch down to shoot up. Pharoah even offered to tap and plug him.

"No thanks," Kenny replied. And as soon as the girl was in his vein, Kenny lost all of his faculties and awareness of his whereabouts in the world.  Pharoah inhaled the smell of sour milk and trash from the dumpster in the alley and felt as if he caught a rat in a trap. It was easy for Pharoah to slide Kenny into the back of his car.

Kenny started to melt out of his high to find himself tied to a chair in a white room.

Kenny nervously asked Pharoah, "What's up, man? Why am I here? You think I owe you money?"

Pharaoh shook his head no, angered by the question.

"Small world," Pharaoh responded.

"What you talkin 'bout?" Kenny asked.

"You know Paris is like a little sister to me," Pharaoh informed.

"Oh my God man, please, she's lying." Kenny's response pushed Pharaoh's anger beyond the boiling point. Pharaoh picked up the bat and hit Kenny's leg with all his strength. The bone cracked.

"I did not know she was your sister," Kenny Whimpered.

"Nobody wakes up on a Tuesday and decides to become a pedophile. Pharoah coldly responded. "You must have done this before."

Kenny begged, "PLEASE, PLEASE, PLEASE." He noticed Dr. Abishai Malcam who was sitting in the corner. Abishai did not move. He was fascinated by Pharaoh's rage. It made the doctor's nostrils flare, the more bones he heard crack.

Kenny's screams were intoxicating to the doctor. The more Pharaoh hit Kenny, Abishai invited the spirits down to join the feast and heard the worship of screams. The aroma of rage was delicious to them. When Kenny's face was unrecognizable, and his lungs started to fill with blood, Pharaoh pushed his chair backward and pulled out what was left of his teeth. The two gold ones were extremely important. He took the tooth extractor Dr. Malcam gave him and rocked back and forth cracking and pulling until the teeth were free. As he ripped them out, he said, "This is for Paris!" Pharaoh was exhausted. As he got up, the blood dripped from his hands to the floor. Dr. Malcam rose from his seat and nodded at Pharaoh. As he began to walk out of the lab, Kenny grabbed for him in fear.  He begged Pharaoh not to leave him with Dr. Malcam.  Kenny screamed through a mouth full of blood.

"I know I'm gonna die. Please, can you kill me, not him? What he does to people is not right." Pharaoh pushed his hands away and walked out of the lab reserving all of his compassion for Paris.

Paris' mind was running as night turned into morning. Paris was so sore it hurt to blink. She sat up and walked to the bathroom and pain ran through her whole body. She looked in the mirror and her eyes were black and blue and swollen shut. She looked at the little slits that were her eyes. Her lip was busted, and she felt scratches all over her face. The rug burns that were healing on her legs rubbed against her sweatpants, and the inside of her mouth had sores where her teeth had sunken through. Tears fell from her eyes. She did not know what day it was and crushing loneliness rushed in.

She sat on the floor holding her legs to her chest and could not stop crying. Day turned into night again. She watched the lights from cars bounce on the walls in the room. Grandma Jessie would bring food up to the attic, but Paris could not eat. The only thing she wanted was the blue pill that helped her forget, feel better, sleep, and stopped her from seeing his face and replaying that day over and over.

Paris did not know exactly how many days she spent in the attic, but she finally decided to descend the stairs as soon as the foster kids who lived in the house left for school. Her world had changed just that quickly. The air was heavy now. She looked out the window in the living room and regular people walked by but all she could see were monsters outside. As she walked down the hall, the cat crossed her path, and she was flooded with fear. In the kitchen, she managed to open the fridge and pour water. As she drank, she could not help but notice that the water tasted different too.  Her whole life was colored by what happened to her. She started to cry again. Miss Jessie called from down the hall,

"Paris is that you?" Grandma Jessie asked.

"Yes, Ma." Paris said in a weak voice.

Her own voice was strange. Miss Jessie walked in and hugged her.

"Why me Ma?" Paris asked, and Grandma Jessie did not attempt to answer. She just rocked Paris back and forth and hugged her until tears came to her own eyes.

After a while, Grandma Jessie led Paris to the living room, motioned for her to sit down, and turned on the TV. Grandma Jessie sat and Paris lay her head in her lap as they stared at the people on the screen. Paris watched but did not see them and realized she was upstairs for three weeks. She drifted into sleep as Grandma Jessie oiled her hair. Paris jumped in fear when she heard keys in the door. Miss Jessie reassured her,

"It's ok Paris! You're ok. You're ok!"

It took Paris a moment to stop screaming and realize that she was with Grandma Jessie and that she was safe. Pharaoh entered and Ma Jessie motioned for him to be still. He did not move as Ma Jessie tried to calm Paris.

Paris did not want to see Pharaoh, but she was glad it was him more than anyone else. Pharaoh did not know what to do and waited for Ma's instruction. He did not like seeing her in this condition. He felt his anger for Kenny rising again. After Paris acknowledged that she was at grandma's house, she calmed down and sat back on the couch. Pharaoh sat in the single chair, and they all watched TV in silence.  Pharaoh made sure not to look in her direction.

"I'm going to get started with dinner," Ma Jessie announced.

Paris and Pharaoh sat in silence. "Can you come with me on the back porch?" Paris asked, breaking the silence.

"Yeah," Pharaoh walked towards the back door. "Ma, we are on the back porch!" He told Grandma Jessie.

"Ok, I'm right here if y'all need me," she responded.

The sun hurt Paris' eyes at first. She looked around the yard and her eyes landed on Grandma Jessie's blue bottle tree. She walked over to the tree and let the blue light from the bottles fall on her skin. Pharaoh was trying to contain his anger as he looked at her healing face in silence. Her thoughts were racing with a million questions. *Where is my mother? Am I going to run into Kenny again, did Grandma Jessie call the police, why did this happen to me, why did I go back to the house alone, Am I going to be scarred forever?* Pharaoh walked over to the tree and let the blue light from the blue bottles fall on his skin too. "I have something for you." He said and handed her a sock with something inside.  She emptied the contents into the palm of her hand, and four ivory teeth with drying skin and two teeth covered with gold comforted her. She recognized

Kenny's two gold teeth immediately. "Monster Killers!" He confirmed. She hugged Pharaoh and the air was easy to breathe again.

<u>8</u>

## <u>Pharaoh and the Issue of Blood</u>

Whenever he saw the scar under his arm, he remembered Paris and how she saved him. Pharaoh always positioned himself in the middle of the house. He had a view of the front door, but the front door did not have a view of him. He did not keep the money in the same place as the product. Two dudes were posted at the front and the back door and had heat. And no matter what, the doormen did not retreat. The middle men blasted whoever got hit by the front men and in the back were lookouts.

Pharaoh and Moses were positioned in the middle of the house in the kitchen on the second floor. Pharaoh measured one gram for every seven grams of coke then poured the cocaine into the pan with baking soda and waited for the bubbles and whipped it furiously. He pressed down the bubbles until they manifested into a cake and then cooled it down with an ice bath.

Moses and Pharaoh did not talk while they weighed, cooked, cooled, cut, and bagged. The first two came in the door and everything went in slow motion. Pharaoh heard them put the gun to the trigger man at the front. "Get down niggah," a voice he did not recognize yelled. He heard Maze get knocked down on the floor followed by a gunshot released by Black. Black shot at them again and then hid behind the wall in the living room to save Moses and Pharoah time to leave with the supply. Black was quickly subdued by them. The intruders released shots and hit Black in the face with the butt of the gun. "Where's the money niggah you know what this is!" A stranger demanded.  As Black fell on the floor, Moses and Pharaoh ran upstairs to the third floor and threw the bags out of the window into the window of the house next door.

Next, they heard the blasts from the middle of the house and knew they had less than a minute to jump from one house to the other house, then run down three flights of stairs into the pitch-black basement and out to the yard.

They ran down to the basement and there Moses and Pharaoh stood back-to-back and heard footsteps coming down the stairs. Pharaoh saw what looked like hot coals come out of Moses' gun. It was up to him to open the door and get them out.  As soon as he opened the door, they both ran. They knew the way like the back of the hand. First, get over the fence and then cut right and run through two backyards. Pharaoh could not help but notice two of the followers also knew the way. He ran opposite Moses. Moses asked, "Nah niggah, where you going?" Pharaoh pulled his piece and let off two shots towards the followers. The followers let off one shot and hit Pharaoh.  Moses and Pharaoh were separated, but the followers were now lost. Pharaoh could not breathe and now he felt hot blood dripping, rushing down the side of his body. He noticed himself walking slower and slower in the dark. He lay down on the cold grass and felt the hot blood contrast the cold ground. He saw smoke rise from his wound, and he felt thirsty. His mother appeared with her soft smile. He did not want to go back to this memory, but he went back in time to the small room where the small boy lived.

He remembered his little body was cut and she was trying not to make a sound as she cried and wiped his wounds. He imagined her there with him at that moment doing what she always did. She attended to his wounds but left her own. Her eyes almost had swollen shut and one of her teeth was missing.

Pharaoh released that memory and snapped back to reality. He saw his breath flow in and out of his mouth. He felt his toes getting cold and then he heard whispering, so he closed his mouth. He felt footsteps on the ground near him, but he was protected by the darkness, so the two-gunmen walked by him. Hot tears ran down the side of his face and into his braids. "I should have died a long time ago," he said to himself and laughed.

Then the memory came back. His mother with the disfigured face looked over his body. The cuts, old iron marks, and the patch of pink skin on his leg from where his father burned him were vivid in his mind. She loaded the gun. He remembers hearing the rumbling from the living room that sounded like thunder; the sound of furniture breaking. His mother was standing and waiting. "He's never gonna let us go but he will never hurt you again," she said.

As soon as he walked into the room, she shot him in the chest. The first shot did not stop him. It only startled him. He started moving closer to her in anger, so she raised the gun and shot him in the head. The sound was so loud his ears ached immediately.

His father's blood looked black in the dark room. Pharaoh felt his heart racing the same way it was racing right at that moment in the cold. Then he remembered his beautiful mother turning the gun towards her own temple and squeezed. He could smell the cats, cigarettes, and the smell of alcohol from his father's body, and he recalled his mother's wide eye stare. The look on her face haunted him and that was what he could see at that moment.

Pharaoh was alone in the dark, laying on the ground bleeding out. He put the gun to his head and pulled the trigger and nothing happened. He had to remember, see, and feel. Pharaoh had nobody to punch or sex, nothing to smoke or drink, and nothing to ease the pain. He lay there for hours it seemed. He dragged himself closer to the street from the yard. He heard snow crunching getting closer and closer to his body. He thought to himself. "This is it, they got me!" As the person moved closer to him he realized it was not them.

"Paris?" Pharaoh asked.

"Shhhhh." She grabbed his coat by the shoulders and dragged his body. He could feel snow gather in his boots, and his legs were scratched over rocks and snow and bushes. She hoisted him up and put him in the car. His breathing was shallow like each breath was his last.

She drove him to Dr. Abishai Malcam's house where Miss Jessie was waiting. They ripped off his clothes and Pharoah slipped in and out of consciousness. When he was conscious, he was aware of parts of the procedure, like a light in his face, a tube in his throat, the sound of the bullet being pulled out, and the pain.

Pharaoh remembered Dr. Malcam's face appearing while his hands were repairing his body. He recalled Paris and Grandma Jessie rushing around the room and then everything went black.

Pharaoh woke up in a dark room, and it hurt him to take in a full breath of air, so he breathed shallowly.  Dr. Malcam was in the corner.

"You almost died," Dr. Malcam said. Moses looked up and opened his eyes wide to try to stop himself from crying.

Moses looked at Dr. Malcam because he knew when somebody wanted something.

"So, you think you saved me?" Pharaoh asked.

"I'm not sure." The doctor retorted. "Did I save you? You came here with a bullet in you and now it's gone."

"Humph!" Pharoah proclaimed. "I am assuming that you did not help me out of the kindness of your heart and that your help was not free."

"You wanted to die, didn't you?" The doctor asked. Moses stared straight ahead and didn't answer the question.

"Well, it looks like fate would have it another way; If you can't live for yourself then what about Miss Jessie and Paris?" Dr. Malcam asked.

"Where are they?" Pharaoh inquired.

"They're here. The doctor confirmed. "I just want to make sure you understand some things before you see them. Miss Jessie is worried sick about you. Paris ran right out the house to look for you when they heard the shots."

"Humph," Pharaoh laughed sarcastically.

"You had a blood transfusion." The doctor said matter of factly.

"Really?" Pharaoh asked sharply.

"Yes, you received a lot of blood. The blood you received was not ordinary." The doctor explained.

"What do you mean?" Pharaoh asked with alarm in his tone. "I didn't give you permission for that!" Pharaoh protested.

"What are you going to do, go to the police and tell them somebody tried to steal your drugs, and you got shot and the doctor who saved your life by using unauthorized blood?" I just need you to give me information about somebody you are connected to, that's all. Whenever you link up with Paris just come here and let me draw your blood, that's all I ask." Dr. Malcam pleaded.

"I'm not doing that," Pharaoh said with an attitude.

"I can quiet those voices and stop those visions." Dr. Malcam assured.

"What do you mean the blood is not ordinary?" Pharaoh questioned.

Dr. Malcam explained. "Well, it carries spiritual information. I need to know about somebody in the future and you are connected to Paris and the spirits told me Paris is connected to them. It's not going to harm Paris at all. It's only going to help me figure out who the person is.

"I think you're cooked." Pharoah responded after staring at Dr. Malcam for a minute.

"I am cooked, but I also have a cure for you, you can stop seeing your mom like that. The doctor promised.

Pharaoh questioned, "How do you know what I see?"

"Because I can see what the eye can't see." Dr. Malcam guaranteed. "Do we have a deal?"

Pharaoh shook his hand. "If it doesn't work, then our deal is over."

"It works…guaranteed!" The doctor reassured Pharaoh.

Paris and Grandma Jessie walked in with food.

"Well, that's my cue to go" expressed the doctor. Pharaoh, I'll be back to check on you.  Pharaoh, Grandma Jessie, and Paris sat and ate together.

## 9

## Double Dutch

The bride walked down the aisle with delicate precision towards a groom with stars in his eyes. While Marlon watched the bride walk, he couldn't help but notice the spine bones peeking through the close-fitted fabric of a woman three rows ahead of him. As the groom made his vows Marlon examined her neck because it revealed itself from behind her shoulder-length hair. He traveled down her back with his eyes landing on her small waist that expanded into a full round coke bottle shape. He was intrigued by her movements and adored how she rubbed her neck slowly while the bride recited her vows. She fidgeted with her shoe and jewelry and occasionally looked around. Marlon kept his eyes on her, catching glimpses of the side of her face, and found himself with butterflies at the thought that she was going to turn around and look at him.

After the vows, people gathered to greet the bride and groom and Marlon tried to keep his body in close proximity to the beautiful mysterious woman. He didn't plan on going to the wedding, but his parents forced him. "You can't just stay in the house for the rest of your life. You have to get up. You're coming with us!" his father said. *Marc and Rebecca are family friends and nice enough people.* Marlon thought as he got ready. He was so glad he decided to attend, for he discovered a reason to go to the reception. He saw his friend Tony and his wife talking to her and quickly walked up to them.

"What's up man?" Marlon said while giving Tony the full slap hands and pulled in for the embrace.

"What's up? Long time no see. What you been up to?" Marlon asked.

"Nothing, just doing what I do, working hard." Tony responded.

Paris started walking towards Tony's wife Cynthia and Marlon gestured towards Tony. Tony picked up on his cues and said, "Paris, this is Marlon. Marlon, this is Paris."

Marlon extended his hand and Paris shook it with no enthusiasm.

Tony's wife asked Paris, "Are you ready to head to the reception?"

"Yes," Paris responded. Marlon watched as Paris followed Tony's wife to the car.

"Who is that?" Marlon enthusiastically asked Tony.

"She's my wife's friend from Binka," Tony confirmed.

"Wow! She's bad!" Marlon expressed.

"You should come out to our meetings sometimes so you can get to know her better." Tony encouraged.

"I'm trying to know her today." Marlon said with sass.

After the cake cutting, speeches, and first dance, Tony, his wife, and the other people who were at her table made their way to the dance floor. Paris also got up so she would not look lonely at the table. She stood near the bar next to the dance floor and checked her phone. She scanned the room and watched the groom Marc and his bride Rebecca look at each other with the deepest devotion. Her coworkers periodically tried to waive her on the dance floor, but she simply made the gesture like she was waiting to buy a drink or as if she were heading to the bathroom.

Paris felt somebody looking at her. She felt him standing beside her. She noticed him too, so she watched him make his way around the room greeting most of the people at the wedding. He participated in air boxing, laughed at jokes, and posed for pictures. She was annoyed by his popularity but had to admit to herself that his broad shoulders and carved form fit perfectly into his suit. Paris knew Marlon was placing himself next to her, so she made herself busy with her phone. She looked up from her phone and prepared to give her nastiest bitch face followed by her cold non-responsive stare as soon as he said something stupid. She prepared a response for all of the questions she thought he would ask. Can I buy you a drink? How do you know the bride and groom? What's your name again? Do you want to dance? Her script was interrupted by Marlon.

"Double Dutch!" Marlon announced.

Paris wasn't sure if she heard him clearly.

"What?" Paris asked.

Marlon continued. "Double Dutch! You know the jump rope game. Before people jump in the rope, they hesitate as they bobble back and forth trying to figure out whether or not the time is right to jump in. If you were a character in one of my stories, that's how I would describe you at this moment.

I would say, the woman stood on the edge of the dance floor the same way she stood on the borderline of life.  She attended the party but did not participate. Her position and behavior at the wedding were a metaphor for real life, 'Double Dutch!'" Marlon said with cockiness.

Paris stared at Marlon with contempt because he thought he figured her out. She was annoyed that he could see her social discomfort and disarmed because she did not have a response prepared for what he said. She rolled her eyes and gently blew air out of her lips.

"Do you always watch other people live life or do you sometimes jump in yourself?" Marlon sarcastically asked when he saw her annoyance.

 She wanted to ask him if he knew how hard it was for her to come out that day? Or if he only knew what it required for her to be in public and be social. Paris decided she did not have to answer any questions at all. She looked him in the eye and now he was disarmed.

Paris replied, "Is that what you do? Walk around making women characters in your book strategically placing them where you want them to be in your world? I saw you position yourself all evening. You think you have discovered all of my secrets; you see me uncomfortable and vulnerable? So now that you see my vulnerability, what are you going to do? You played yourself smarty. The next words out of your mouth better be real because I can tell you're used to making up stories"

 Marlon acknowledged, "I know you're playing Double-Dutch right now. All I'm saying is, jump in!"

She smiled. Marlon smiled. "Do you think you have me figured out?" Pais asked.

Marlon extended his hand and Paris placed her hand in his hand as they made their way to the dance floor. Paris was determined to make him eat his remarks. She was extra sexy and precise in all of her movements. Marlon was intoxicated by her movements. There was a mixture of sweat and laughter as their bodies pulled away and came together, which made time disappear as they danced and laughed. Tony asked Paris if she was ready to leave, but Marlon interrupted and volunteered to take her home.

As they got in the car Marlon said, "I know you don't want to go home, so where do you really want to go? I'll take you anywhere."

Paris hesitated at first, but Cynthia reassured her earlier that Marlon was a good dude, so she said, "Let's eat! I'm starving. The food at the wedding was good but it was not enough."

"Sounds good, come be a pig with me," Marlon replied.

"Everything is closed in Boston now." Paris reminded him.

"Mick e Dees near MelCass is open," Marlon confirmed.

"True, let's go." She said with a smile.

When they arrived, Marlon confirmed her order. "You want a fish sandwich? You want a milkshake and fries?"

"Yes" Paris said and rubbed her stomach.

"I'm going to get the same thing." He confirmed.

After they devoured the food, Marlon asked, "You want to go to Smitty's?"

"Where is that?" Paris inquired.

"What do you mean where is that? Marlon asked with shock. "Everybody in the hood has been to Smitty's!"

"Not me," Paris admitted.

"It's THE after-party spot." Marlon said with certainty. "Where have you been?"

The question was loaded for Paris. She hardly ever left Grandma Jessies' house unless she was working at the Salon.

"Do you want to go?" He asked.

Paris looked at Marlon and that was the first time in a long time she was having fun.

"Sure," she heard herself say. They parked on a street near Nubian Square in front of a huge house.

"Is this your place?" she asked nervously."

"No," Marlon reassured.

Paris relaxed when she saw a group of women walk by and enter the yard. The women were at the door for a few seconds and then they disappeared into the house. Marlon reached for her hand after he opened the car door for her. They were greeted at the door by an older West Indian man with gold teeth and a smile. The rhythmic slow sounds of reggae music blared and everyone in the place who was wearing white glowed. The smoke-filled room was packed with people slowly grinding, laughing, playing cards, and talking.

Marlon gave dap to several guys as they walked over to the bar. "Bourbon, please," Marlon requested.

"For the lady?" The woman asked.

"Can I have a bottle of water please?" Paris responded. Their drinks were abandoned when the DJ let the beat drop on a particular song. The crowd went wild. Marlon locked his fingers between hers and moved to the edge of the dance floor near the corner. He pulled her in towards his body and they danced close and slow. Paris found herself smiling and for the first time in years, she was attracted to a man. Marlon and Paris rotated between dancing, talking, and smiling at each other all night. Marlon helped her respond to Ma Jessie's text messages asking if she was ok. As the crowd thinned out, they decided it was time for them to go as well.

They exited the house at 4:00 a.m. Paris was surprised to see the pink sky with the sun on the horizon. Marlon looked at the morning sun falling on Paris' face in the car.

"This is the most fun I have had in years," she said.

Marlon agreed, "Me too. I've been going through a lot lately and you made me forget about all of that tonight."

"You're so authentic and easy to talk to," Paris added.

"Oh yeah? You're funny. You make me laugh." Marlon complimented.

He pulled up in front of her house. "I would love to see you again," Marlon said with sincerity.

"I would like that too," Paris confirmed.  Marlon pulled out his phone and started to enter her name and then he called her phone.

"That's me calling you so you will have my number." Marlon reminded in a joking way.

Paris leaned over and gave Marlon the sweetest kiss he ever received in his life. Her tongue was sweet in his mouth, and she made his stomach twinkle. Her hand on his face and the smell of her perfume aroused him. This is what moving on feels like he thought to himself, and the possibility made him so happy inside. He walked her to the door.

"I'll call you. Will you answer when I call?" Marlon asked.

"I sure will," Paris smiled.

Grandma Jessie came on the porch and Paris gave her a thumbs up and Grandma Jessie gave her a thumbs up relieved that she was finally able to go out and enjoy herself after all these years. Grandma Jessie walked back in the house and periodically checked the car in front of the house. Paris and Marlon sat in front of the house talking and laughing for hours.

Marlon's happiness was short-lived. Marlon was greeted by his mother when he reached the house. It looked as if she was waiting up all night. Marlon could not tell if she was waiting for him or his father. It was clear that it was for him when he saw the worry on her face and heard his mother say, "Son, I don't want you to be upset." Marlon did not want to hear whatever his mother was getting ready to say. "Did somebody get hurt?" He asked.

"No" His mother said with worry on her facial expression.

"Ok Ma," Marlon responded. "I really don't want any bad news right now." He walked upstairs to his room and fell asleep.

When Marlon woke up, the news announced the marriage of Kern Grant and Sky Jones. "Give me a fucking break!" He screamed. His mother was knocking on the door, but he ignored her. She entered the room without his permission. Her mouth was moving but he could not hear what she was saying. It was like the times when he was under water. His room went red. He looked down at his hands and they melted. He looked out of his window and the trees outside started walking towards him. Everything in his life was fake. "It's all fake!" he yelled!

His father entered the room.

Marlon yelled. "Dad, I'm so glad you're here! It's all fake."

"What's fake Marlon?" his father asked.

Marlon pointed to his mouth. "Our truth is fake. I was your kid dad. A kid. You shouldn't have made me lie. I'm always lying, stuff it down. Stop crying, tough it up, move on!" Marlon could not keep track of his thoughts. His mind was moving fast, fast, fast. He screamed. The floor fell out beneath him. "Help me, please?" He screamed as he scratched the skin off of his arms. His parents were holding him trying to stop him from ripping off his flesh.

"What's wrong with you?" his mother asked and started to cry.

Marlon screamed, "Why aren't you helping me? Do something." Marlon saw the floor coming towards his face fast like a train and just like that he was knocked out.

Paris waited and waited but the call from Marlon never came. Instead, Paris received a call from Master Abishai Malcam. "I have a patient in my care that speaks very highly of you. I was wondering if you would be willing to see him as a part of his treatment." The doctor asked.

"Who is it?" She asked.

"Marlon Green." He responded.

"What happened to him?" Paris asked.

"He's having a Trauma breakdown." Doctor Malcam revealed.

"Oh my God!" Paris expressed as her eyes began to water.

"He asked me to reach out to you. The doctor stated.

"Really?" Paris asked.

"Yes," Dr. Malcam confirmed.

"Why?" Paris inquired.

"I'm not sure but are you willing to come?" The doctor asked.

"Sure, I will come." Paris agreed.

When Paris arrived at the hospital. She was escorted to the locked unit. Marlon was no longer groomed and poised. His hair had grown into an afro and his face was covered with low hair. He whispered in her ear, "Oh my god, I'm so happy to see you. They are listening to us." He told Paris.

Marlon told Paris a series of far-out statements. He told her the moon was following him and that the trees were trying to kill him. He insisted and believed he lived on earth before with a child and a wife. He told her that he committed suicide with his wife in the past when they jumped off the boat that was headed for the Americas from Africa. Paris understood what it was like to be afraid of the world, hurt, and lonely. "Do you want to play cards?" She asked him. He smiled when she asked.

"Yes please." He responded. As they played cards, Marlon's mind slowed down as he focused on the game and the beauty of Paris. The first time in weeks his mind stopped running. Paris stayed until he fell asleep.

As she left the room and walked down the hall, she was summoned by Dr Malcam. He asked. "Can we talk for a little while before you leave?" He walked with her to his office. "Come in please." The doctor invited.

"Can we leave the door open?" Paris asked before entering.

"Absolutely," he responded. "Would you like some tea?" He offered.

"No thanks. What happened to him?" Paris asked. "He had a break. When a person has too much, they break," he told Paris.

"I think your blood can help him. I can make medicine based on his chemical imbalance and your affection for him. The fact that you made such a deep connection with him can heal him. You already know the importance of peace from when you went through your situation. I can make him medicine just as good as the one I made for you."

Paris struggled with herself as she just met Marlon a couple of months ago. Her spirit wanted to run for the door, but her heart wanted to stay. She wanted to see the man she met before, and she wanted to be like Grandma Jessie. She did not want to leave him there. She decided to stand by Marlon.

Over the next four months, she read him a total of six books and donated her blood as Master Abishai requested and the man she met returned and the love grew strong between them. They stayed together after he left the hospital.

Marlon knew Paris was the one from the very first time he saw her. She felt like home to him and his love for her could not be articulated. From the first moment until after leaving the hospital, he was committed to her and would be for the rest of his life. Those were the thoughts and memories Marlon meditated on lying in bed. He remembered how she healed him and they have been together for years now.

Marlon was awakened to the smell of fresh-baked scones and marinated pot roast. As he sat up in bed, he recognized the sounds of a beautiful quiet Sunday morning. He knew he could find Paris in the kitchen. He made his way down the hall and noticed that everything was spotless. Paris left nothing out of place.

As he walked down the hall, he saw the smiles in the frames that resembled them. He knew he could find her in the kitchen cooking with the soft music playing and a smile waiting for him. Her back was turned to the sink, and he decided to watch her as she worked.

When she finally turned around, he was smiling at her. Mornings like that made him happy and forget about all the arguments and problems. He was grateful for all the sacrifices she made for him. "Happy Birthday, baby," Paris sang and kissed him with that sweet kiss that made him miss her.

The roast she prepared was so delicious and seasoned to perfection and the scone impressed him even more. He put his arms around her waist as she passed by and kissed her neck. He was surprised that she was receptive to his touch. He slowly showered her with kisses and led her to the bedroom. Her kisses were so sweet and soft to him. He loved making love to her on the rare occasion it happened.

As he began, he realized that he was not as hard as he was when he was with Sky. He grabbed a quick image from his experience with Sky. He was then hard enough to enter Paris. He rotated the two women in his mind. His goal was to pleasure Paris. He used his memories from Sky to make Paris moan. He was gentle and methodical with Paris. Her pleasure and happiness were his duty. He showered her ear with "I love you, baby."

She responded, "I love you too."

After the sex was started with Paris, he could not switch his entire attention back to Paris. He noticed that Paris had her eyes closed and wondered for one second if she was someplace else too. He came so hard and held Paris so that she could not move. Paris laid her body on Marlon and listened to his heartbeat and fell asleep in his arms. He took the opportunity to caress her back and look at her body freely without her covering herself or maneuvering so that he couldn't see her body.

He looked at her beautiful ass and the side of her perfect breasts and put himself asleep by looking at her body. Marlon woke up before Paris and noticed a cut on the back of her neck. Her skin was red and irritated. Marlon moved her hair to get a better look and saw that it was a cut stitched with red stitches. She was asleep but Marlon woke her with his question.

"Hey. Babe, wake up! What happened to your neck?"Marlon asked.

"I don't know, where?" Paris knew exactly what he meant.

Marlon became immediately annoyed as she rushed out of bed and headed for the mirror. He walked up behind her as she pretended not to see the mark. He lifted her hair off her shoulders and grabbed a second mirror off the dresser. He held the mirror behind her and said, "See, how did that happen?" She looked in the mirror and into his eyes. He stared at her blankly and expected her to answer. She grabbed her t-shirt off the dresser and began to put it on. He hated the fact that she ran to cover her body. "I made a commitment with Master Malcam."

"Why?" Marlon asked with annoyance in his voice.

"Seriously, that's what I choose to believe in. Dr. Malcam helped save you a few years ago, remember? Sky reminded Marlon. "Do I ask you why you believe in the people and things you believe in?"

Marlon replied. "I have every right to ask you why and how you got a scar on your body."

"Well, Mr. Secretive, it is what it is! Why so inquisitive?" Paris asked.

Marlon knew to back off. He did not want Paris to start asking him questions. He wanted to talk to Sky but there was no chance of that happening on that day. Sky would never call him on a Sunday or cross any boundaries that would jeopardize him. He could not explain why she crept into his thoughts at the strangest moments.

Paris was mad at him, and he was annoyed that she came in and tried to act normal. They had been invited to her friend's house and she had to put on airs as if everything were well.

When they arrived at Paris' friend's house. Marlon was so bored kept himself busy as he watched lips move and read wine labels. They drank wine and told jokes. They were questioned. "When are you guys getting married?"

He jokingly said, "She keeps turning me down." He watched her periodically detach and look down at her phone and text someone that wasn't present. All night her fingers would race across the screen of the phone. Her attention was stolen in forty second increments. Marlon watched. He was shocked, surprised, and delighted to get the text Max flashed across his screen. "Happy Birthday." It caught him so off guard he smiled. Even though a male name showed up on the screen, he knew it was from Sky. When Paris saw his smile she asked, "Text message?"

"Did you get good news?" Paris continued.

"Yes, I'm surprised you looked up from your phone to notice." Marlon said as her phone lit up again.

"Whatever", Paris said, embarrassed that her phone was going off at the wrong time.

Marlon revealed, "Yes, this is my first text all day. It says, Happy Birthday. "Do you want to see?"

Paris did not want to interrupt the event, so she resigned to let the issue go because she didn't want to start an argument in front of everyone.

On the way home there was a thick impenetrable wall of silence. Marlon wondered, *how and when did this wall of silence develop between them? Why did they stop having sex? Why are they always bickering? Why don't they touch each other anymore? Why are they so bored? Why are they so mean to each other? How does this happen to two people that love each other?*

## 10
## Glue

**THE TIES THAT BIND ARE PROFANE AND DIVINE THAT WHICH ONE IS SEEKING CAN BLIND THEM FROM REAPING.**

Her grandmother was the first person Paris thought about when she woke up. She remembered laying her head in Mamma's lap in the summertime and her grandmother combing her hair while she hummed. She started to cry.

The door was closed but she heard Marlon in the next room. She knew he was working while trying not to disturb her. She slid out of bed and walked over to her table. She opened the small box and untwisted the plastic bag that held the coarse purple salt. She poured the salt on the wooden square and watched the grains of salt randomly fall into the various carved numbers and symbols. She spread the residual salt with her fingertips then made a circle and removed one small red candle from the box. She took the lighter and melted the wax to make a place to sit the candle in and stuck the candle in its own wax. She looked at the numbers that the salt fell into just like her grandmother taught her, imitation being the best compliment. She knew she was going to have to be strong while she was over Grandma Jessie's house.

She missed her grandmother even though she just saw her yesterday. When she saw her at the Binka meeting it was apparent that Grandma Jessie could no longer hide her illness. Paris was shocked to see her thick grandmother now slim. Paris asked,

"Grandma, do you want me to move back in with you for a little while?" Paris recalled asking her last week.

"I see you everyday and you take care of me, that's enough. Grandma Jessie told her, "I don't want you worrying about me! Pharaoh out, so he gonna stay with me and make sure I'm safe and I'm gonna make sure he stay straight."

Paris sat at her table as she remembered the conversation from last week. Paris assigned numbers to people in her life. When she finished the candle the wax had formed signs in other spaces on the wooden board. The numbers meant "around" but she had no idea what that meant. She decided to ask Grandma Jessie and proceeded to get ready to leave.

Paris let the water run down her back to soothe her. She thought about her grandmother the whole time she was in the shower. She got out of the bathroom, thinking, *I'm not ready to lose her*.

As she approached the living room, she looked at Marlon's organized confusion. He had piles of paper on the floor. He also had his notebook, tablet, phone, and television running. Paris sat on the corner of the couch not wanting to disturb Marlon's maze. The television was on a very low volume, and they were both called to attention when Paris spotted Sky on TV.

Paris watched Marlon squint his eyes while looking at the TV. Paris sarcastically stated, "Awe, your friend!" Paris searched for the remote control to turn up the volume. Marlon watched her listen to the news clips of Sky. The reporter said Sky was going to be sent to answer questions from the Ethics committee. Paris shook her head in agreement with the news coming out of the TV.

She said, "Wow, some people just can't take responsibility for their actions. People like her leave children unprotected."

"Paris you don't know what happened. You're listening to one side of the story, and you don't have all of the details." Marlon defensively retorted.

"I know that kids are getting abused and there is a diffusion of responsibility. Nobody wants to take the blame. They just want to look the other way. You can't look the other way when it comes to children. These people say they want to help. These so-called non-profit organizations pop up every day. They know these kids are being abused and leave them with families that neglect, starve, beat, rape, and use them as benefit babies and take the checks to buy drugs. The social workers go to those homes and let the kids stay in toxic destructive environments. When is it going to change?" She asked.

Marlon had a thousand things he wanted to say but could see that Paris was upset. He held his thoughts and could only utter, "Wow, you don't even know her. I can't believe you are being so judgmental."

"Apparently God already judged her!" Paris said in disagreement. Marlon's defense annoyed Paris. She stood there staring at his shocked face.

Paris interrupted their staring competition and announced. "I gotta get out of here. I'm going to my grandmother's house."

"Yeah, that's a good idea," Marlon encouraged, "because I can't believe what you're saying right now."

Paris rushed back to the room, and she brushed her hair into a ponytail, slipped on her black leggings, a wife-beater, a sweatshirt, and sneakers. She left the house within ten minutes.

Grandma Jessie was so excited to see Paris even though it had only been a few days. When Paris hugged her, Grandma Jessie held on and cried, and Paris had no choice but to hold on and hug back. Paris watched her walk around the kitchen still trying to be a good hostess. She offered Paris ginger tea with biscuits and then tried to start cooking a full course meal. Paris instinctively started helping. "I'm not a guest here! I'm here to take care of you, not the other way around." Paris reminded her. Grandma smiled and sat down.

As they cooked, Paris asked Grandma Jessie questions she already asked her a million times before, just to keep Grandma Jessie's mind off of the cancer. Paris asked how to make her biscuits fluffier, ribs juicer, scones, lamb, and Ma was so happy to share. Paris knew how to already because they had years of bonding together in the kitchen. But Paris was happy to see her grandmother delighted when she repeated her stories and recipes. Paris listened intently to the stories about discounts at the store and Dr. Abishai Malcam's teachings in Binca as if it were her first time hearing these things.

"Ma, the numbers and symbols I got this morning gave me the word "around." What does that mean?" Paris asked.

"That is a very complicated combination of numbers and symbols." Grandma Jessie answered. "There may be some time where you sit in confusion, and it can also mean completion. But the thing about *around* is that its meaning will remain unclear until it reveals itself. "

After they ate lunch, Paris could see that Grandma was getting tired as they played cards at the table, but she didn't want to run out of time to get the latest update from the doctor.

Paris asked with apprehension."Ma, how did everything go this week at the doctor?"

"I was tired after chemo as usual,"Grandma Jessie confessed.

"So, how did Pharaoh do, taking care of you this week without me?" Paris asked.

"He did a good job. He cooked for me, even though I couldn't eat. He cleaned, went shopping, and made sure I took my medicine. I was scared he was gonna knock one of the doctors upside the head though." Grandma Jessie laughed and continued. "He doesn't like to hear bad news about me and he was asking for you," Grandma Jessie confirmed.

"I wasn't ready to see him," Paris answered.

"I just want to know that the two of you will take care of each other." Grandma Jessie expressed. Paris took Ma Jessie upstairs and helped her bathe. She greased her scalp and braided her hair the way Grandma Jessie did for her when she was a little girl. Paris oiled Grandma Jessie's skin and put on her night clothes even though it was the afternoon.  Paris turned on her judge show and they both lay in bed  and watched her show until Grandma Jessie fell asleep.

Paris walked downstairs with Ma's dishes.  She opened Pharaoh's room door and scanned his minimal belongings. Four pairs of the latest sneakers. A stack of jeans with tags, shirts, and a watch. A picture of Mamma, himself, and Paris stuck on the dresser mirror. Paris walked into his room and noticed it was cooler than the rest of the house. She walked in a little further and inhaled his smell. The rain outside made the room look gray. She turned on the light and walked over to his dresser. The weed was buried under his socks and underwear and laid on top of handwritten notes from the past.

Paris recognized her own handwriting from when they were kids. The days when he was sick, and she went to run errands. She sifted through the notes that read, "Hey stupid, here's your food, stop leaving the toilet paper roll empty," and she smiled to herself. She turned around and tried to grab the air back into her mouth, her heart started to pound, her body jerked, and fear gripped her when she realized she was not alone. Pharaoh was standing at the door watching her look through his stuff.

He stared at her and did not speak one word. Her heart was racing. It took her a few seconds to register that it was Pharaoh because that was not how she remembered him. Pharaoh towered over her and looked down into her eyes. His dark copper skin was smooth, and his hair lay on his face in perfect lines. His lips were full and complimented his perfect white teeth.

"You scared the shit out of me!" Paris said with the fear still in her voice.

"You scared cuz you didn't come see a niggah!" Pharaoh confronted. His voice was deep and slow. He playfully grabbed his weed from her hands and pulled her into his arms. "You're still a thief huh?" Paris could feel his hard body as he bear hugged her and lifted her off of her feet.

"You caught me!" she replied.

"Damn right" Pharaoh interrupted. "I caught you! You were trying to steal my BLACK BETTY!" Paris laughed nervously as Pharaoh took off his jacket. She could see his muscles flex under his shirt as he breathed. He turned on the TV and sat down on the stool next to his bed.

"You can have some. Sit your ass down!" Pharoah jokingly instructed.

"I don't even know what to say," she said.

"What can you say? I caught you!" Pharoah said confidently.

"I'm not talking about being caught in your room. I'm talking about me not coming to see you while you were in there." Paris said sincerely.  He thought silently to himself almost as if he were visiting a memory for a moment. He looked at Paris from the side of his eye, dumped the weed on the brown paper, pushed it back and forth, and started to roll.

"You got me through even though I didn't hear from you. You saved me. I replayed it over and over in my mind." Pharaoh stated.

Paris sat on the floor next to him and started to explain, "So many things have changed. I don't even know where to start." Her beautiful big eyes smiled at Pharaoh even though she was being serious. He already knew about her and how her life changed.

He didn't want to hear about her new life with her man, so he interrupted,

"Why are you tripping?" He asked Paris.

"We both agreed that you were going to get out of here. Nobody knew I was gonna get caught up." Pharaoh knew Paris was thinking about the secrets the two of them shared. He reassured her, "The money you put in my canteen was real. Anytime, anywhere, anything and it's just between us. Let the bones stay buried."

As the smoke in the room got heavier Paris and Pharaoh could feel their senses heighten. Paris felt the weight of her eyelids and heard cars drive on the wet road outside. She felt the cool wood floor under her feet contrast the warm temperature of the room. Paris put Pharaoh totally at ease. He laid back on the bed and realized there was no other place he wanted to be. Pharaoh occasionally tapped her arm or leg between his sentences. He realized he tapped her hard. "I better not tap you too hard; I know you like that rough shit!"

Paris rolled her eyes and smiled, "That's in the past." She was hoping he had forgotten about the incident from when they were younger. His humor put her at ease. She loved not having to watch her grammar or worry about being questioned about her ideas. She could speak easily and say whatever she wanted. Paris and Pharaoh lay side by side smoking and laughing.

"Damn this is the Paris I know. You were talking all proper and shit. I was wondering if a little of the old you was still in there or if you disappeared completely." Pharaoh joked.

"I'm still here." She reminded him.

The aroma from her lip balm was left on the tip of the joint and the little wetness from her lips turned Pharaoh on when he pulled in. He could not help but notice her thick thighs and caramel skin. He looked at her as if he were her man and owned the right to look at any part of her that he wanted. Paris could feel his eyes walking up her body. "My mind was going crazy when I was in jail. They had me trapped like an animal. I got sent to the hole a lot and I thought about you. I thought about you almost every night." Pharaoh confessed.

"I could never see you like that!" Paris declared. He sat up and pulled up his shirt. His stomach muscles and chest were covered with beautiful feathers and tribal symbols.  Paris saw her grandmother's face and her own name permanently carved into the skin over his heart. She traced her name with her hand. Although he seemed calm, she felt his heart pound hard and fast as he stared at her. He watched her eyes grow watery and he knew he moved her. He lay back down on his side and she turned her body on the side to look him in the eye while he talked.

Pharaoh felt a sense of peace that only came from Paris. She knew every dark dirty secret about him and loved him anyway. He convinced himself whether subconsciously or on purpose that she felt something too.

She returned home without her man and entered his personal space, looking through his stuff. He lifted the chain he gave her five years ago and traced it with his finger and said,  "I can see I wasn't the only one thinking." The back of his hand touched her breast a little and he placed his hand behind her neck. "Come here," he said in a low whisper voice. "Come here."He repeated as he pulled her whole body close to him with ease. His kiss was warm and strong, his tongue tasted like cashews with a hint of smoke.

Paris felt like she was on a swing every time his tongue entered her mouth, and she inhaled his aroma. He slowly moved his hand up her shirt and touched her nipples. His muscles tensed as he kissed her slow and strong. She wanted his hands all over her body. She gave him permission and confirmed his touch by moving closer to him. His strong hands moved around her curves, and hands roamed down to her waist and thighs. His big hands could not contain the thick fullness of her curves.

He felt the wetness between her legs. It was dripping between his fingers and that was when she snapped out of her moment. "This is bad. I gotta go!" Paris said and slid off of the bed and moved to the door, but Pharaoh was right behind her. She saw a light under the door from down the hallway. She knew she was wet, and she knew it was her last chance to escape the situation.

Pharaoh was right behind her. He gently pulled her by her wrist back towards him. Paris did not resist. Pharaoh slowly slid his hands down the back of her leggings and removed them with one thrust, caressing her thick thighs and watched her legs and ass jiggle as the pants came down. Paris couldn't breathe. He turned her around, picked her up, and put her on the dresser. He slid her wife beater up and sucked her huge nipples. Paris thought about trying to stop him, but she did not have the strength to even stop herself. Paris unbuttoned his pants as fast as possible before she could think about it and touched his penis with her hands. Paris felt the heat rising off his body. He was big, strong, hard, and hard. He wanted her to want him. He wrapped his hands gently around her neck and said,

"I won't go any further until you say you want it!"

He tightened his hands a little more around her neck the way she liked it, and she said, "I want it."

"I can't hear you. tell me" Pharaoh coached.

She used the little strength she had left to push him inside of her body. Pharaoh did not thrust right away; he enjoyed her muscles contracting and the wetness of the inside of her. He filled her slowly, being aware of his own size. He wanted her to admit she liked it. Pharaoh grew harder when he saw her eyes roll in ecstasy. He felt her get wetter. Her legs felt soft wrapped around his body.

Paris' body was in a state of perfection. Pharaoh was hard and strong inside of her. He whispered in her ear, "Only you." She moved her body closer to him and he went deeper. She arched her body into him as she grabbed his hips and pushed him deeper into her body. Her legs gripped his open straddle as the dresser began to shake. Paris felt so good to Pharaoh. He lost concentration for a moment and loosened his grip. She quickly placed her hands on top of his hand that was around her neck, reminding him to squeeze harder, "I trust you." He lifted her off the dresser by her neck and ass and placed her on his hardness, forcing her deeper. She was now perfectly subdued the way she liked to be.

Paris wrapped her arms around his shoulders and held on. She started to grind and bounce on him. He whispered, "I got you!" Paris was captivated by his strength that was holding her in the air. She could not see or breathe. Pharaoh listened as she inhaled and held her breath. He knew her silence meant she felt good. He slid back and forth in and out of her. He tried to rub as much of her sweat on him as possible. She was only inhaling now and when he reached the spot Paris could not take it anymore. She exploded. All of the air and sound she held in, filled the room.

"Ah, ah, ah, ah," She erupted so hard she started shaking and making sounds that were music to Pharaoh's ears.

As Pharaoh gripped her, he said, "I know how you like it, get it!" Pharaoh held her until she finished but she motioned for him to put her down. He gently put her back on the dresser, and she slid off and she quickly picked up her pants off the floor, pulled down her shirt, and ran out of the room towards the front door. Pharaoh pulled up his pants and followed her to the front of the house. Paris ran out the door to the car and Pharaoh watched her run away.

As she left the porch, cold rain hit her face as if she was splashing a drink on her to bring her back into reality. She looked up and saw Pharaoh in the doorway and pulled away so fast.

She drove several blocks before she pulled over. The rain was so fierce and violent she could not see out of the windshield. She stared into space and watched the raindrops hit the windshield. Her heart was pounding so fast. She yelled, "This is a problem, this is a problem, and this is a problem!" she banged her hands on the steering wheel, and then buried her face in her hands. The fierce rain would not let anyone see inside the car. She became hysterical. The tears running from her eyes came down as fast and furiously as the rain outside. Paris panicked.

*"What the fuck just happened?"* She asked herself. *"What am I going to do?"*

Paris wanted to be angry, but her heart and body would not allow her to lie to herself. She had flashes of Pharaoh slipping in and out of her and how he sucked her nipples so good. She felt dirty for liking to be choked. She realized she still smelled like Pharaoh and that she was still wet.

*"I have to tell him. I can't tell him!"* Her heart was pounding and she had to admit to herself while no one was watching and while the rain was hiding her that she felt more alive than she felt in a long time. Pharaoh was going to be a problem.

She watched the raindrops hit her windshield, cried and stared down the street into space. The tears, her panic, and hysterics slowed down. *"I have to tell him,"* she resolved. The radio was on during her panic attack but Paris did not hear it until the news on the radio interrupted her train of thought. The news about Sky came on and annoyed the shit out of Paris. She was instantly irritated again and did not know why.

Marlon's face appeared on her phone followed by his ring tone. The sound quickly brought her back to reality and focus. His face went blurry as the silent tears fell from her eyes. Paris had to change the tone of her voice before she answered the phone.

"Hey, what's good?" Sky nonchalantly answered Marlon.

"How's Miss Jessie?" He asked.

"She's good," Paris confirmed.

"Are you coming home soon?" Marlon asked.

"Yes, Did you get a chance to pay the cable bill?" Paris asked as she tried to sound normal.

Marlon answered, "Yes, I did. Are you still mad at me?"

"No! let's forget about all that" She remorsefully suggested.

"I would like that!" Marlon replied with softness in his voice.

"I'm on my way. I'll pick up dinner from Italia's." Paris promised.

"Ok, you must really forgive me. You know that's one of my favorites." Marlon teased.

Paris hurried, "Ok, I'll see you when I get there."

"I love you," Marlon affirmed.

"I love you too," Paris responded.

Paris ordered their food and went to the bathroom while she waited. She pulled a stack of paper towels from the roll, wet them, and added soap. Then she prepared another stack of just wet paper towels. She brought all her supplies into the handicap bathroom stall and washed between her legs, under her breasts, her neck, behind her ears, her lips, and her face. She repeated until she wiped Pharaoh's scent off her body. She exited the bathroom and retrieved her order before she went home to Marlon.

## 11

## What I Hate I Do

## War Against the Law of My Mind

Marlon looked at his hands on the steering wheel and felt the sweat forming on his palms. His heart started beating faster as he drove down Washington Street past the library and into Codman square. He tried not to focus on what his mother was going to talk about. He occupied his mind as he watched people laughing and shopping. A few people stood outside of the store where they played numbers and sistahs walked out of the nail shop. Men stood on the corner talking and brother Malcolm the neighborhood entertainer danced with his cowboy hat, shaking his legs spinning, and then presented his hat for an offering.

Marlon felt his throat tighten as he swallowed and turned onto Melville Ave. The busy, loud street immediately turned into a tree-lined quiet street in typical Dorchester fashion. He inhaled deeply as the car rolled down the peaceful street and approached the huge orange and brown house with perfectly manicured lawn and bushes.

He parked and looked at his face to make sure nothing was out of place. His face was oiled, his haircut fresh, and his collar was sharply ironed. He took inventory of his clothes as he walked up the walkway. Crisp white shirt, tan slacks, brown shoes. Marlon hoped his mother would be pleased. He hesitated before knocking on the door and instinctively looked up to his childhood window. He remembered the nights he spent alone as a child in the big house. His mother opened the door. "You're late!"His mother barked. He opened his arms, and his mother presented her cheek and then rolled in for a hug.

Marlon followed his mother even though he knew his way around every nook and cranny of the house structure. His mother had changed the furniture and the color of the walls. He took a moment to soak in the new style. He looked at pictures of his mother, father, and himself. He looked at the younger version of himself in the picture frame. His eyes were sad even though his smile was big. Marlon felt his own loneliness radiating off the picture. The smell of curry chicken, rice, and beans danced in the air and interrupted his thoughts. He was excited about the feast that awaited. His mother yelled, "I'm going to check the pot. I'm coming!"

Marlon took off his shoes and walked around. He knew his mother cleaned the house by herself. The beautiful hardwood floor and tall ceilings made the artwork that adorned the walls more stunning. He truly could not find one piece of dust. They sat in the dining room and saw that his mother had extra China, crystals, and silver laid on the table.

"Are we expecting more people?" Marlon asked.

"Yes, but not yet," His mother said as she slowly looked Marlon up and down.

"Are you taking care of yourself?" She asked him.

"Yes, Ma," He answered.

"Why do you look so slim? His mother said in a judgemental tone.

"You think I'm slim?" Marlon asked.

"Yes, too slim," his mother replied.

Marlon looked at his beautiful mother and noticed the gray hairs and small lines on her face that he did not notice there before. "Marlon, you stayed away too long. You need to come and see us more." Marlon thought it was strange that his mother always used the word us when she referred to herself and his father.

"Yes, I agree I should come to see you more." He resigned.

"I don't want you to say that and the next time I see you is six months from now." His mother persisted.

"I'll do better, Ma," he promised.

"Speaking of doing better. How is London?" His mother asked sarcastically.

Marlon leaned back and crossed his arms. "You mean Paris?" He corrected her.

"You know who I mean! Is she doing something with herself or is she still living off you?" His mother questioned.

"Here we go, Ma!" Marlon said with annoyance in his response.

"She needs to be doing something to contribute. If the two of you are going to be together, you need someone that's not just a pretty face but also a partner. You need someone you are compatible with who you can pay bills together, get along, and make a life. You come over here and you look so slim! The last time I came to your house it was a mess. You need someone to look after you. Take care of you. Most importantly, I need grandchildren!" His mother unapologetically expressed.

Marlon stared at his mother and slowly nodded and blocked out every word she said from that point forward. A skill he learned from childhood. He knew that all he had to do was vocalize an "Uh huh, I hear you" every couple of minutes to appease her as she talked. Marlon's eyes traveled to all the beautiful things in the dining room and the parlor starting with his mother. Her light brown eyes, shoulder length hair, and caramel skin, dressed in her silk Kimono dress. The antique leather silk and mahogany couch. The oriental rug and lamps, but he could not find the beauty of happiness anywhere.

His mother continued, "We worked hard because we wanted you to be better than us. I never wanted you to have to struggle as much as we struggled. We sacrificed because we really wanted things to be easier for you."

SACRIFICE! Marlon thought to himself. Marlon wondered if his mother knew that he *knew* just how great her sacrifice was. He remembered the fights and heard the arguments. There was one day they all died. He lost his mother, father and himself. He learned don't be honest, stuff it back down, don't cry, lie, and please others. The day he heard his father tell his mother, "I don't want to be with you anymore. My soul is dying in this relationship. You don't know how to love me. You're cold and unaffectionate." His mother crumbled. She showed her love through cleanliness, cooking meals, motherhood and she was at that moment going to lose the love of her life. His mother did not know how to hug, dance, let loose, and smile. She had been hardened by paying her way in this world. Studying, working, cooking, cleaning, sacrificing. He had never known his mother to cry but she cried that day, and he believed that was the day his mother died.

She became the wife who settled for an unemotionally available provider. She looked the other way and allowed his indiscretions. His father stayed out of devotion. Marlon became invisible that day and at the same time overprotected. His mother focused on every outer aspect of him. The friends Marlon chose were not worthy enough to be around him according to his mother's standard and so his friends were selected by his mother. He had to be driven and hand-delivered from one location to another. He had to attend private school and was enrolled in music classes. It was all about the image because he was his mother's refuge. Marlon was lonely and trapped. He was the thread keeping his parents together. He looked at his mother and her things and wondered how she could help him.

"Hold on Marlon, your aunt is on the phone!"His mother said as she handed him the phone.

Marlon was so happy that his aunt called. It snapped him out of his memories.

"Marlon, go help your aunt bring in the food." his mother commanded.

"Yes Ma?" Marlon hurried to help his aunt bring in the food.

"Oh my God! You're so fine! Look at my nephew!" Aunty Susie saved Marlon so many times he recalled. Her house was freedom. He could go to the corner store, stay up all night, eat candy, wrestle with his cousin, get wild and funky without taking a bath, and without her, he would have never had any freedom. She hid his secrets and never told his mother. He and his cousin were brothers and wild boys at Aunty Susie's house. He could see Aunty Susie was starting to tear up. "If your cousin was still here, he would be right beside you, you know!" Aunty Susie reminded him.

"I know Aunty!" Marlon gave his aunt the kind of hug that held her up at the same time. He felt her hot breath on his chest and just held her. His mother walked in and was lost as if she didn't know what to do. The loss of his cousin was another reason his mother smothered him.

"You look fat Susie!" His mother said in a playful tone. Aunty Susie burst into laughter. Marlon was relieved. The sisters were notorious for friendly banter. They were united in overcoming hardships like many black women that were free to tell each other the cold hard truths and laugh. Aunty Susie turned around and retorted, "At least I can cook you know; somebody has to do the cooking around here."

Marlon walked upstairs to his room as his mother and aunt caught up. He was surprised to see everything was the same. His mother did not move anything. Marlon spent so many hours in that room writing and dreaming. "Hey, son!" Marlon heard his father's voice behind him.

"How's it going?" His father asked.

Marlon reached for his father's hand, and they pulled each other in for a hug.

"Can't complain," Marlon responded.

"Did you like the computer I sent you?" His father asked.

"Absolutely," Marlon said appreciatively. "I love it!"

His father held his hand over his heart and asked. "How's Paris?"

"She's good!" Marlon said, shaking his head up and down.

"Where is she? His father said and looked around to see if she was there. "She was invited to come."

"You know Ma and Paris don't mix." Marlon said with certainty.

"I know, but if she's the one, they're going to have to mix. Your mother has a way of getting her way in case you didn't know that by now." His father warned.

"Paris is my choice and Ma has to understand that I'm never leaving her." Marlon confirmed.

"Well, there it is then!" His father agreed.

"You need to buy some property soon my son, if you plan on making commitments like that. God is not making any more land. There's no reason for you to not have real estate security." His father declared.

"Yeah, I'm going to buy something soon." Marlon resolved.

"We can help you with the down payment." His father offered.

"Roxson," his mother called his father from downstairs.

"Coming!" Roxson responded. "I'm going to see what your mother wants. We'll talk later."

"Ok, I'm going to my old room for a little while." Marlon said and gestured toward the direction of the room down the hall.

"Ahem! his father cleared his throat. "You mean my room. You don't have any land in this house. His father joked.

Marlon loved his father but held contempt at the same time. His father was both the hero and the villain. Here he was larger than life. He was the man who taught him how to ride his bike, taught him to swim, and taught him to build things. Also, he was the man who made him wait in cars while he visited his mistresses and made him lie to his mother. He pushed for him to be an attorney even though he wanted to be a writer.

There was tension between the two of them as they exchanged little words. Marlon felt as though he was the reason his father stayed in an unhappy relationship. Marlon never worried about tuition, or how he was going to buy his first car. He did however wonder what his father would be or who he would be if he left his mother free to be and do what he wanted. His disappearance would not have been strange or questioned at all. Those actions happened in Dorchester every day.

Once in his old room, Marlon laid on his bed, placed his hand over his chest and wondered when his heart was going to stop beating fast. He stared up at the painted mural of the universe on the ceiling. He opened the nightstand table and was so excited to find old notebooks. He breathed in and out deeply. He looked at the airplane puzzles he completed when he was young. The framed awards for science, debate, and math.

For a moment he felt like he was sinking into the water. He was cold and began taking in salty water. He had to turn quickly and start stroking so as to not sink any deeper. The waves were impossible and high and then he saw her. Instinctively grabbed for her and caught her hand pulling her back up to the surface. She breathed and cried, and he looked into her eyes. He told her, "Kick your legs" in a language he did not understand. The woman kicked her legs, and she stopped sinking. He looked up. There was a huge boat nearby. They were holding each other and kicking. The sun was blazing, and the water was freezing cold. Marlon was awakened by voices downstairs. No longer in the ocean, no longer cold, the most real dream he ever had. He walked downstairs shaken by the dream.

He followed the voices into the garden to eat. Glasses glistening in the setting sun. He poured himself a glass of wine and joined the table. His mother, father, auntie Susie's husband, and two neighbors greeted him with a smile. Marlon's father began grace.

"Heavenly Father, we thank you and praise you on this glorious day. A gathering of family and friends. Where two or three are gathered. You are present. We are grateful for all that you provide. We ask that you bless this food and the hands that have prepared it. In Jesus' name Amen."

Everyone responded, "AMEN,"

Aunty Susie stood and raised her glass. "I would like to give a toast to my handsome nephew for his most recent accomplishment of winning the Carol Brown Community Service Award. Congratulations on your award, nephew." Marlon looked at Aunty Susie and bowed his head in acknowledgment.

"When were you going to tell us?" Marlon's mother asked.

"Well, it is kind of hard to talk about yourself." 'Hey everyone, I'm great! Marlon responded.

"So humble, I'm proud of you son." His mother confirmed.

"Thanks, Ma." Marlon appeased.

Marlon's father smiled, stood up, and shook his son's hand. "Not bad, for someone who was supposed to be an Attorney." Marlon smiled too.

Aunty Susie said, "Please tell us about the award."

Marlon explained. "Well, Carol Brown was a woman who never received an award for the things she did. She was a single mother of seven. She raised her children and kids that were not hers and loved her community. She served her community silently and helped so many people. The award however is based on the fact that she had a dream in her heart. When she was a little girl, she wanted to become an artist. Her teacher told her that she wouldn't make any money and that she should do something else. She believed her teacher and went on to have those children but the dream did not go away. She started painting when she was 60 years old. Her paintings were quite beautiful and showcased the inner beauty of a single mother and seeing the world through her eyes. One of her daughters decided to create an award in lieu of the tombstone so that no one would ever forget her mother. I am receiving this award because they said that my journalism, and social media channels, have impacted our community in a way that honors her memory." They all clapped.

"Congratulations!" they chanted.

The rest of the evening was full of smiles, stories, and laughter. *Not bad once you get past the other stuff Marlon thought to himself.* He got a text from Paris that ended the evening. The text read, "I'm finished, can you pick me up?" Marlon hugged his father, kissed his mother and auntie Susie on the cheek, and walked to his car. Marlon was worried about his dream from earlier in the day. It was the same woman from the past.

Marlon felt drained as he drove to pick up Paris. He spent a whole day with his people and danced around the real issues. He believed that the phony life and avoidance is one of the reasons he snapped. He drifted back in time to the days after he broke up with Sky. Marlon remembered how he lay in bed for thirty days straight. He hoped she would call or answer his calls. He kept rewinding their conversations and thoroughly reviewing the good times and the bad. He masturbated to their memories and convinced himself that they would get back together. Another week passed by, and he missed his plane to Italy.

One day ran into another and he would get lost when trying to remember what was said in simple conversations. His parents argued the way they always did. The arguing did not help him.

"The boy just needs to toughen up; he's soft!" he heard his father say repeatedly. Marlon felt like he was having an out of body experience. He found himself pacing and he couldn't catch up with his thoughts. His hands were right in front of him, but he couldn't stop shaking. He watched his hands as they were pulling all of the items out of the fridge, and he could not stop his hands.

He found himself trying to be normal. That was when he started seeing people he did not know. Whenever Marlon went to sleep he was living in another time period, living the life of a man in Africa. The man had a wife and Marlon was trapped in his body. The man's wife blamed him and yelled about the death of their child. He saw a baby that he could not save. It was as if Marlon and the man were the same person. He tried to comfort the man's wife the best way he could but she was inconsolable. The man and his wife were captured by enslavers and the man and his wife were sold into slavery. Marlon found her one more time on the ship and she told him that she wanted to die. Then she said to him, "I've lost my baby and now I've lost my home. I can't bear it."

He looked at her and said, "Let's be free," and they jumped. It was so cold that Marlon could not shake the cold from the ocean. The cold would not leave his body. It was the continuous complaints about the ocean and the cold that made his parents think something was wrong. Marlon avoided sleep because he did not want to live this man's life.

His parents took him to the doctor with the invisible notes and invisible medical records. The one who accepted payment off the books. The one with the side door everyone in the hood knew about. The one that performed secret surgeries and abortions. He kept the secrets of the rich and the poor. The one that cremated bodies in secret and made ailments disappear. Marlon's father "the judge" and his mother did not want anyone to know about Marlon's breakdown. They admitted Marlon to Dr. Malcam's facility for treatment.

*Romans 7:15, 23*

*I do not understand what I do. For what I want to do I do not do, but What I hate I do…But I see another law at work in my body, warring against the law of my mind and holding me captive to the law of sin that dwells within me.*

## 12
## How Great Is That Darkness?

Sky tried to call the store several times but no one answered. She tried to look up the address on the Internet for directions but nothing came up. She even tried to see a satellite image of the store but no such location existed. She decided to drive from Charlestown to Dorchester. It was foggy and chilly outside and hardly any traffic on the road. Sky had no idea how it would play out so she prepared herself to wait outside but the store was already open when she arrived.

She sat in her car and breathed in and out to get the heaviness off her chest, but it would not go away. She inhaled deeply and held her breath and attempted to hold the air in and remove some of the heaviness. Sky finally got the courage to get out of the car and looked inside the store for movement. She entered and the aroma of the store was warm and spicy. She remembered to enter and wait from the last time she had gone with Sharon. Her eyes looked at the shelves stocked with orange, yellow, pink, white, green, and black candles. Carved saints with African features stood behind the counter next to a row of beads. Her eyes stopped traveling around the store when she saw the blue vase full of beautiful long-stemmed yellow roses that she did not expect to see.

Love emerged after a while and at that time Sky was determined to appear respectful and humble. She said, "Good morning sir. I'm sorry to come here so early and unannounced but I was wondering if I could have a moment of your time." Love remembered her immediately and was not pleased to see her. "I'm seeing visions in the middle of the day, having bad dreams and spirits that I used to see when I was a little girl are talking to me. I don't know what's happening. I'll answer any question you have. I just really need your help." Sky confessed. Love started unpacking a box and it was almost as if he couldn't hear her at all. Love started walking away. "Please sir, please!" Sky begged.

"I can't help you. Talk to my daughter." Love said dismissively.

"Is she here?" Sky asked.

"No." Love barked.

"Is it ok for me to come back? When will she be here?" Sky asked with desperation in her voice.

Loved walked into a back room and closed the door behind him.

Sky did not know what to do. She waited in front of the store hoping Solace would come but she did not. She called Marlon.

"Hey Skit," Marlon answered.

"What are you doing?" Sky questioned.

"I'm getting ready to board my flight. Are you good?" He inquired.

"Yeah." Sky reluctantly responded.

"I'll hit you back when I get settled."Marlon confirmed.

"Ok, safe travels." Sky replied.

Sky drove around aimlessly hoping that she wouldn't have another vision. She wanted to be around people and found herself at the mall spending money. Sky looked out of the door of the store she was in and saw Solace pass. She dropped all of the things she was going to buy and started speed walking towards Solace.

"Hi Solace!" Sky said as she nervously approached Solace.

"Hi," Solace squinted her eyes and reluctantly answered.

"Your father was really mad at me the last time we met,"Sky reminded Solace.

"Yeah I know. He doesn't like people that much and sure didn't like you. He thought you were smug."Solace confirmed.

"I'm not like that at all." Sky reassured Solace.

Solace interrupted. "I know you're not. I can tell. You also needed help."

" Wow, thanks for saying that," Sky said with relief.

Sky tried to calm herself by looking down at the floor. Sky moved closer to Solace and lowered her voice to a whisper. "It's really hard to tell someone you just met that kind of personal information."

"Do you think he will see me again?" Sky asked.

"Probably not. I think he's all set with you."Solace said with certainty.

Sky felt her stomach drop and her mouth started watering as if she was going to throw up. She searched Solace's face and there was silence for a moment.
"The visions are getting worse. Can you help me?" Sky pleaded with Solace. More silence followed as people drifted by them in the mall. As they spoke Solace could feel her feet heat up and her body sway ever so slightly and she also heard multiple voices.

Solace finally said, "There's a lot with you. I don't know if I can help you or not."

"Please, I need your help. Will you try?"Sky pleaded.

Solace looked at Sky sternly and said, "You have to be open and believe in God. If you don't believe, then we can't help you."

"I really want to believe but this is all new, to be honest with you." When you say believe, believe what exactly? The only thing I know for sure is that the visions are real and I know something is wrong. I believe that. I'm ready to listen. Is that enough?" Sky asked.

Solace looked Sky in her eyes, at her posture, and clearly, she was a different woman than the one who visited the store.

"Ok, I'll try." Solace confirmed. Sky's face loosened and her breath became lighter.

"When will your next cycle start?"Solace asked.

"My cycle?"Sky questioned.

"Yes, your period?" Solace repeated.

"I think in three days."Sky responded.

Solace wrote down an address on a piece of paper and said, "I will take you at our house. So, in three days I will see you at 3:00 a.m."

"3:00 a.m.?" Sky repeated to make sure she was hearing her correctly.

"That's the time."Solace confirmed

"Thank you. I'll be there." Sky promised.

The three days seemed like an eternity, but Sky was eager to find out what was happening.

On the day Solace arrived at 2:45 a.m. It was quiet and the street was deserted. Each minute closer to 3 a.m. was like an hour. She wondered if that was really going to help her. The air was starting to get cold and she could feel fall in the air and observed as summer leaves turned into beautiful orange, red, and brown.

Sky approached the house and stopped. The porch and windows were painted blue. It reminded her of her mother. She walked up the steps, onto the porch, and looked at her phone which read 2:58. She stood there with plans to knock at 3:00 a.m., but at three  Solace automatically opened the door. Sky stepped in. The house was warm and welcoming. Lamps lit the living room to the right and stairs were directly in front of them. Solace seemed very relaxed almost like she was high.

Solace handed Sky a white bathrobe. "I need you to change into this."

She then handed her an alabaster bowl. "I need you to put your jewelry in here. Let me know when you're finished." Sky started to ask questions about the jewelry, but Solace already left the room. The thought of Sky's blade in her purse in close proximity was her only comfort. She tried to beat back her fear of being in the house totally naked with those people she did not know. She had to remind herself that her visions and dreams were real, and she wanted answers.

"When you finish let me know," Solace said from the other side of the door.

The room they entered next was beautiful. It was warm and smelled like licorice.

"Please sit here," Solace pointed to one of the chairs near the tub. There was a copper tub in the middle of the bathroom and spices were laid around the rim. Solace started placing the spices into the water and instructed Sky, "Put your hands in." Sky put her hands in the water and Solace asked, "Is it too hot?"

"No," Sky responded.

"Ok, please get in." Solace instructed. Sky felt like her tongue was being touched by a square battery as she climbed into the water, but the heat comforted her. "Everything you need to fix this situation is already within you. I am simply here to help," Solace said to Sky.

Solace placed her fingertips on Sky's eyes and reminded her.

"The last time we spoke you said you were having visions in the middle of the day, and you were seeing a woman running but you don't know her." "Is that still true?" Solace confirmed.

"Yes. It happens anywhere, even if I am driving. I can feel her fear, her heartbeat, and her sweat. All of these visions started happening recently when a little boy named Preston died at the Maker's House." Sky disclosed.

"Yes, I saw that on the news," Solace acknowledged.

"So, what do you think this all means?"Sky asked.

Solace responded. "We are going to find out. I am going to start by asking you some questions. As you speak, God is going to reveal things. I will be able to see between your words. It will either tell me the intentions and desires of your heart, events from the past or future or see and hear what we can't see and hear in the physical. It is different for each person. I never know what God is going to reveal or what is going to happen. The more honest and transparent you are, the more I can see."

"Are you a psychic? Sky asked.

"Absolutely NOT!" Solace denounced emphatically. "I believe in the Father, the Son, and the Holy Spirit."

"Ok," Sky said as she eagerly shook her head up and down.

Solace continued. "Tell me what you were thinking when I asked you to tell me what's happening. The very things that you were thinking about will make up the circle of connected events.

Sky responded. "I thought about the day I was taken from my mother. I waited hours for her to come home but she never did. As I waited for her, I got scared and decided to hide in the closet. While I was in the closet, what seemed like ghosts started to surround me. I ran out of the closet and my living room transformed into a forest. The forest my mother and I made and colored to put on the wall had manifested into real life. The spirits chased me out of the closet into another room, but they stopped. I instinctively bowed. I could not bow low enough to the ground to honor him. God said, stop running. That was the same day the police removed me from my mother's custody. I wanted nothing else to do with God.

Sky continued, "Monday I was sitting at the coffee shop and a forest started appearing all around me. I sat with my coffee. The coffee shop slowly turned green. The music stopped, the birds started to chirp, the air became thick and heavy, and a woman ran by me. I keep seeing a woman running. I don't know her. This is not a dream. This is happening when I am awake. I was confused because I thought I was having a flashback to when I was a girl running in that room. I realized this was something else. I tried to remain as still as possible and finally, the Barista at the coffee shop asked me a question and the forest disappeared. I'm scared because my mother used to see things. I'm afraid it's happening to me."

Solace put up her hand to indicate that she had a question. She asked. "So, were you seeing these things before Preston died?"

Sky continued. "Yes, I did when I was about twenty-two. My best friend and I took a trip to Rome. As I was in my room that night, I saw what looked like water on the floor. I looked in the water and saw a man and some kind of a deal was being made. The next thing I knew I thought I was on fire and I was running around naked in a park in Rome and my best friend found me."

The information was coming to Solace so fast that she wasn't sure if she could articulate what she was seeing. "Are you only having visions when you are awake or are you having dreams too?" Solace asked.

"I'm having dreams too but I'm not sure if I'm dreaming or if it's the daytime because it's all starting to run together." Sky responded.

Solace stopped. "I want you to come out of the water now. Dry yourself and put this oil all over your head and body and put these garments back on and let me know when you're finished."

Sky called out to Solace after she finished putting on the oil and said,

"Ok, I'm done." Solace walked back into the room and motioned for Sky to sit on the chair across from her.

Solace began to ask, "There is a baby buried in St. Michael's cemetery. Who is the baby?" Sky lowered her head almost as if she was taking a moment of silence as she remembered the beautiful baby girl before she said,

"That's my baby girl, she died. I used to be married."

"How long ago was that?" Solace asked.

"It was twelve years ago." Sky replied.

"What is the dream that you keep having?" Solace asked.

"I dream about the red room." Sky confirmed.

"Can you tell me about the dream?" Solace asked.

Sky explained, "Yes. There are beings in this realm that seem to feed off the perceptions in my mind. I fear spiders so spiders appear. I'm afraid of heights so everything keeps elevating. There are bugs that jump high, crawl upside down, shape shift, and reduce or increase their size. The hallways are lined with gold and the floors are marble. I started running and noticed a hammer in my hands. The hammer enabled me to latch on to railings, light fixtures, and helped me to climb.

I was afraid of a presence and suddenly I was chased into the stairwell and kept running. At the end of the corridor, the door was hot when I touched it, but I pushed it anyway and it led to an elevator. I took the elevator to a lower level of the church and when I got off there I ran to another floor. The hallway I ended up on was painted in rich black and gold. Beings were looking at me as I ran but I did not care. My running did not seem unusual or alarming to them. Which made me uneasy?

I turned the corner and slowed down when I saw an endless hallway of doors. I chose a door and entered one particular room and suddenly everything was red and gold. Gold was intricately laid on top of a red wall with all kinds of carvings and symbols. I immediately thought the room was beautiful and that I should not be in here with shoes. I removed my shoes and followed the ivory-colored path to ivory steps and at the top of the steps, there was a gold throne.

The floor where the throne was placed was glass and below it was filled with emeralds, diamonds, and gold. As I studied the riches on the floor, I noticed a small gold woman buried in the floor with something next to her. I was unsure if it was a leg or some other limb.  A closer inspection led me around the door, where I was able to see other riches like human hearts, livers, tongues, ears, and eyes. I was creeped out so I began to slowly back out of the room. I noticed that the woman was actually a baby and there was a blood line.

I realized this was a place I did not want to be.  I backed out of the room faster. I was being chased. On exiting the room, I ran down the hall and entered a lower level sanctuary. The sanctuary was painted black and over decorated with dimly lit old fashioned bubble shaped lamps.

A choir was rehearsing a song in a tongue I did not recognize. The beings on that lower level were wearing white silk. The beings made me nervous because I was running and out of place and my terror did not move them at all.

They just returned to what they were doing.  I kept going lower and found a heavy huge door. I pushed the door and entered a section where the people looked emaciated. I noticed they were wearing burlap sacks and sad looking clothes. They were working in some kind of field. There were slaves above with what looked like a tornado of water that would suddenly spew down on more people in the fields. A few of the enslaved saw me running and they were the first to acknowledge me for the first time.it had door monitors. Somehow, I got i

I kept running until I came to a shoreline and got in line to take a boat. I decided not to go any further into whatever that place was. One bald headed man saw me leaving and he decided to leave with me.  When she started heading to the two big doors, they started to close. The bald black man and I got there in time, and I am not sure if we were passing through physical doors or some type of spiritual vortex door.

The four people that came through with us were still wearing the clothes. We were all standing in the sanctuary. The man was dressed in a headdress and was a priest of some kind. He was riding on air and had a sleigh or chariot of some kind led by dogs. He started ordering those who came through with me to be recaptured and two of the people were seized and taken away.

I sat down and tried to blend in so the man that was trying to recapture them would not mistakenly think I belonged with them. The guy with the bald head sat four seats away from me and tried to blend in with the other beings the same way I was trying to blend in. The other people were recaptured except her and the guy with the bald head. At the end of the sanctuary was a forest. He looked at me from the side of his eye and motioned for me to run. We both ran into the forest. The forest was familiar to me. My mother had described it a million times to me as a child.

"So, what do you think this all means?" Sky asked Solace when she finished describing her dream.

Sky found that she was starting to become more comfortable with Solace.

## 13
## Hearing

Solace looked at Sky and told her, "Your dream is about a spiritual place where spirits live. It's like a holding spot. These spirits are captive. In this holding place, spirits can be summoned from there."Solace said, "Your spirit is tied with spirits that lived in other people before you were born."

"What does that mean?"Sky inquired.

"The spirits that lived before are not at rest. You have something in common with them. These we refer to as familiar spirits." Solace confirmed.

"So, what happened to the spirits that lived before?" Sky asked.  The information was coming to Solace so fast she wasn't sure if she could articulate what she was seeing.

Solace began to speak in tongues, "Atta Come Shalla Vit mMa oolS ode Nnnamen ssssltool Fotool bbbbiiina llaba che veen llllf sek. Lhaboon tok vim sin Jabba te Kool no Zebool!". Sky was uncomfortable when she heard Solace speak in tongues. *"What is this?" Sky thought to herself.*  The information that Solace was receiving was moving at top speed. At first, Solace could not articulate what she saw to Sky. Solace was only able to speak in tongues. Solace had to slow down so that she could speak the words in English instead of spirit.  Solace asked, "Did the man in your dream resemble anyone you know?"

"Yes, Marlon!"Sky confirmed.

The more Sky talked the more Solace could see. The people were becoming clear. Their bones grew flesh and muscle and the people started to come into focus and gain color.

Solace began to explain to Sky what she saw.

"There are four people." Solace confirmed.

"What people?" Sky asked.

"People from the past." Solace responded. These people actually lived before. It was a long time ago.

"Are they my ancestors or something?" Sky questioned

"No." Sky reassured.

"What people then?" Sky asked again.

"Listen very closely. I am going to tell you everything I see," Solace explained.  "I see three friends that grew up together in a royal house. Dakarai, Tuma, and Bala. These three children were extremely close.  Tuma was the female heir to the throne. Dakarai and Bala were children of servants.  As they grew into adolescents, Dakarai followed Tuma everywhere and protected her so fiercely he was inducted into the royal guard. Bala was a gifted and skilled seamstress for the royal family. Dakarai and Tuma engaged in fierce arguments and then they would come back together and laugh. Observers saw how Tuma and Dakarai started to stare at each other. Tuma spent hours and hours confessing her love of Dakarai to Bala. Bala carried a thousand secret messages from the two lovers. The kingdom whispered as word spread that the princess was in love with a lower class. Dakarai and Bala meant everything to Tuma; she loved them both. She was in love with Dakarai. Although he was a servant, his strength and manliness could not be denied. His stature was tall and strong, his eyes were amazingly strong and beautiful. The three were inseparable until Bala's mother the queen heard Tuma refer to Dakarai and Bala as friends which meant equals in her mind. The queen observed Dakarai's affection for Tuma that she had not previously recognized and was filled with disgust. She announced Tuma's marriage to Sabra who was a prince from another kingdom. The queen also decided that Dakarai and Bala should be married. Tuma was so upset by the marriage arrangements. Tuma expected Bala to refuse to marry Dakarai. Bala was terrified of the queen and would never resist her demands. Bala and Dakarai were joined by the elders of the village. Her face was cut with Dakarai's family markings and both shared the same exact pattern.

Tuma was filled with anger and rage. She was so devastated she could not bear it. Her mother made sure she did not show her feelings and sent Bala and Dakarai away for two years. Tuma did not know where they were sent.  Tuma was married to a weak man who was given to her so that her father could remain on the throne and grow in power and also be king of the neighboring village.

Dakarai was devastated when he learned that he could not be with Tuma. As time passed, he started to fall in love with the quiet, soft, and kind spirit of his wife Bala. They formed a strong bond. Dakarai's reputation grew as he led the king's guard. He was ordered back to the kingdom. Tuma rushed to see him. Their hearts pounding as if they were never separated. When he arrived, Tuma was obsessed, and he grew in confusion.

On one hand, he was in love with Bala and also with Tuma. The women were two opposites. Bala was a simple village woman with no comforts. Tuma however was the first-born daughter of the king.

Tuma's blood flooded with jealousy when she saw the love in Dakarai eyes for Bala. She became ill in desperation for all of his love. She sent her husband Sabra away to spy on the rumored ships on the shore line. She ordered Dakarai to have sex with her.

The Shifter welcomed the king's daughter to his house.  She explained her love for Dakarai and the situation with his wife and promised her that the price for his love would not be cheap. The Shifter explained, "He will be committed to you and he will love you but you must promise me that you are willing to pay." Tuma found herself making a deal. "I need you to make an inner vow and give me a sacrifice of blood." The Shifter explained. Tuma did not hesitate. She was more than willing to give him her blood for Dakarai. The Shifter explained, "Your blood would be too easy. I need you to get innocent blood on your hands. Bala is pregnant with Dakarai's baby. The shifter insisted.

"I need the baby's blood and bones to feed the spirits. As long as the innocent blood cries out from the ground, the spirits will allow Dakarai to be yours." The Shifter promised. Tuma did not know how to maneuver that but she decided that she needed help, an accomplice.

The Shifter knew that her agreement to that would get him a more powerful position and unleash spirits that would feed his god. He was excited but wasn't really sure if Tuma had the heart to carry that through. The Shifter instructed, "The next time you have sex with Dakarai catch his sperm, spread it on your garments, let it dry, and carry it to my house. Make sure you speak into his ears, make sure he eats something, scratch his back, try to get skin and blood under your nails, ask him if he loves you and make sure he makes an inner vow with his mouth. To ensure we have covered all the gates that need to be open.

His unfaithfulness to his wife will ensure proper spiritual entry. Once we have access to him, we will have access to his wife. If he agrees with you in any way with his mouth, the spirits will have legal entry and claim to the baby."

Tuma recruited her own husband to seduce Dakarai. Sabra negotiated his promotion. He was chosen to be a royal guard to the king and when the king fell asleep he was summoned to the bed of the king's daughter. Dakarai was offered a space in the king's house for the delivery of his child with the best midwives known to the kingdom. Bala's mother urged her daughter not to deliver their child in the king's house. Bala's mother stated, "The king and his family are not good people." However, Bala loved Dakarai and he only needed to imply a thought to her and Bala complied.

Bala saw her beautiful baby girl emerge from the womb with a cry so strong that it flooded her heart with love and pride. The next thing she noticed was the sorrowful face of the midwife as she walked the baby girl to the door. She thought she heard the voice of Sabra. She got nervous and began to ask for Dakarai. "He is on the way," said the midwife. Bala knew something was wrong when she asked several times for her baby girl. She tried to get up only to be held down by the midwives. Dakarai walked into the room with a silent blanket and tears pouring down his face. Bala was breathless and her heart was automatically filled with pain. Bala yelled, "That is not our baby, Dakarai! I saw her. That is not our child." She let out a scream so long, loud, and devastating that every person that heard her cry was pierced with the sound of heartbreak they would never forget. "Bury me too!"Bala cried.

Sabra returned to the Shifter's house and handed the beautiful baby girl to Tuma. The baby was perfect and beautiful and Tuma found herself staring off into space and then into the baby's eyes. She hesitated for one moment as she saw Dakarai in the baby girl. Before she could think anymore the Shifter asked, "How much is love worth?" Tuma reminded herself of her purpose and handed the baby to the Shifter. The Shifter twisted the neck off the baby and dissected the arms, legs, and torso and placed it on the makeshift altar. The Shifter moved so quickly Sabra threw up and knew that he had done something deep, dark, and evil.

Tuma ordered her guardsmen to capture Bala and send her to the slave ships. Tuma did not count on Dakarai fighting for Bala. He fought with all his might. He bashed in the head of the first man to touch his wife and the brains lay on the ground. He was eventually overtaken and was subdued by the king's men. Five of them he had eaten with on numerous occasions overpowered him and knocked him out. He awakened Bala and himself in chains captured by men that called him brother.

When Tuma realized Dakarai had been captured She was filled with anger. She arrived at the Shifter's house. In tears her mind was like scrambled eggs and she was blinded by rage and months of examining her thoughts over and over again. Exhausted from staying awake. Her voice was hoarse from yelling for hours. Daikarai and Bala had been taken to the ships. She arrived at the house of the shifter. Some of her royal guards were grieved with fear and refused to go into the Shifter's sanctuary. Six of the royal guards entered with the princess. The shifter sat tall on his altar surrounded by blood, bones, hair, and teeth. The princess sternly said, "You promised me that Dakarai and I were going to be together and he would love me."

The shifter was in an altered state as if he were drunk. He had just finished consuming spirits. Tara yelled, "Answer me!"
The Shifter responded, "our deal is still good I assure you. Your love will prevail but it's better because it will be for eternity.  Familiar spirits will be able to execute love again and again. I assure you he is yours forever.
Tara was inconsolable and her blood boiled. She could feel her temples thumping and her heart beating fast. Her tears and snot ran into her mouth and Tara yelled.

      "I wanted him to love me now! you did not tell me this before. She pulled her hair out of her head and scratched her own skin off of her neck.  You  tricked me. Do you know what I have done!! Do you know what I have done!" Tara screamed. The shifter smiled at her. He replied, "I gave you exactly what you asked for." His calm demeanor overwhelmed Tara. She stopped crying, she clenched her teeth together so hard they began to chip. Her chest was moving up and down. She pulled the knife out of the back of her dress and plunged it into his heart. He smiled again and laughed, "Ha, ha, ha, ha, ha, ha, ha ha, ha, ha, ha, ha," Her guard backed up one step.  She pulled the knife out of his chest and plunged it again into his stomach. His hot blood ran on her hand. He confidently confirmed. "This is only flesh my dear." His blood stained her face as he spoke.  Tara did not stop stabbing until her guard pulled her away from his mutilated flesh.

After Solace finished explaining what happened in the past she sat in silence for a minute in disgust. Finally, Solace said, "I am thoroughly disturbed."

"Me too." Sky agreed. I have to admit this is a little far fetched. If I wasn't experiencing this myself I wouldn't believe it either."

"I think it's easier for people to believe in the things that they can see with their eyes. Solace remarked.

"So, what now?"Sky asked.

Solace explained, "You have to ask yourself, who is closest to you that has access to your blood? When you find out who is close to you then think about how you are tied to them. Sky told Solace, "I am not close to a lot of people. Only Marlon really."

"Well then!" Solace confirmed.  He is connected to this.  The two of you have a sexual connection so he has access to your blood that way. Also, there are more people connected to this. You need to find out who they are. Most importantly, there is a person that is summoning and **feeding** those spirits from the past. What I saw tonight is very specific. Whoever that person is knows you and they know a lot about you.

Sky confessed, "Thank you, I don't feel as crazy now.

"You're not crazy, this is real. Solace confirmed. As a matter of fact the next time the forest comes up and you see flies. Do not swat the flies away.  The flies are covering something they don't want you to see. They can't hurt you."

## Matthew 6:22-25

New International Version (NIV)

[22] "The eye is the lamp of the body. If your eyes are healthy, your whole body will be full of light. [23] But if your eyes are unhealthy, your whole body will be full of darkness. If then the light within you is darkness, how great is that darkness!

## <u>14</u>
## <u>Evil in the Heavenly Realms</u>

Sky was comforted after the meeting with Solace. She went home and remembered Solace's instructions. "Do not swat the flies because it feeds the demon baby gnats. The flies are blocking a door." Sky went in the shower and when she came out flies started to fill her bathroom. Sky stayed still and did not swat. Instead, she began to place one foot in front of the other. As she walked, the flies started to clear a path and slowly started flying away. Sky took another step. The cool earth felt good under her feet.

She looked up at the rich green canopy and strong streams of sunlight burst through and occasionally hit her face. She breathed in and the air was moist and warm. Somewhere buried in Sky's memory was this path in the forest. The forest was oddly familiar now. She asked herself, "How did I not remember?" Sky and her mother made this place when she was a child. Sky and her mother stayed awake all night and painted their entire apartment green. They spent hours painting and cutting out paper trees, water, sky, birds, and a road. They made animals out of construction paper, animals that were mixed with humans and other beings. The forest was beautiful. They ate nothing but cereal, cookies, chips, and ravioli all weekend.

The same path she was on led to a river. She kept walking to the river. Sky was so happy she started crying and remembered and started laughing. She heard a voice singing with the sweetest melody. "If you're lost, stay still. If you're lost, stay still. If you're lost, stay still. She followed the voice to the river, and the woman in blue was there.

She stopped. It was her mother. She was washing a baby. Her mother placed the clean baby in a basket. She was cautious as she approached. Her mother turned around with a baby that had radiant brown skin that was illuminated by the sun. "You found me! I knew you would come." Her mother said confidently.

Sky screamed from her belly, "Ma! Ma! Ma!" And cried. Her mother grabbed her, and Sky curled up like a little girl. Her mother said, "I have been waiting for you for a long time." Sky was rocked back and forth by her mother and tears dripped on her dress.

"Is this real? Sky asked. "I mean is this place real?" Her mother answered, "You're in a spiritual place baby. This is a realm!"

"Realm?" Sky repeated.

"Yes, but you are safe in this realm. I tried to tell you as much as I could when you were little. Your angels are here. Nothing can hurt you here. You are special. I always tried to protect you when you were little because spirits were always trying to get you." Her mother reminded her.

Sky shared, "I keep seeing a woman running. She is appearing in the middle of the day. I don't know her, but I can feel her fear as if she is me."

"Running is not good. Her mother warned. "There's definitely a spirit or a demon after or attached to you."

Sky continued, "Before I came here, flies were everywhere."

"Flies?" Her mother repeated and her facial expression filled with worry.

"Yes, everywhere." Sky confirmed.

Her mother explained, "Yes, that is Baby Gnats. He's a demon. He's a strong demon. That means something has been working on you for a long time."

"Why?" Sky questioned.

"It's all about your purpose. Your purpose must be great. If you want to know why, ask God what your purpose is." Her mother responded.

"Why does the forest keep appearing?" Sky asked.

"The forest will only appear when you're in danger. her mother reassured. "It is protection for you. There are other spiritual realms that are not good. You must remember that there is also evil in the heavenly realms."

"Evil in the heavenly realms? What does that mean? Sky questioned.

Her mother explained.

"That means good and evil are side by side for now. As much as there is good in the world, evil is right there. The evil ones have the same access and power as the good ones. We have to fight. In the Bible Job was the subject of conversation between God and the devil. He was able to conversate with God in the heavenly realm about Job. Then the things that were discussed in heaven were executed on earth. Whatever is happening to you on earth started in another realm. As Jesus taught us to pray 'Thy kingdom come thy will be done on earth as it is in heaven.' What do you think that means?" Her mother questioned.

Sky gently protested,

"Ma, I'm not a spiritual person. I try to stay away from that stuff. I don't read the bible. You're speaking another language to me right now." Sky's mother stared at her for a minute.

"Some things are true whether you believe them or not!" Her mother enthusiastically stated. "You have a gift.

Nothing is wrong with you. The gift is being revealed to you is all. You have to find out about your gift. Your gift is your purpose and the reason you were put in the earth realm. You have a physical purpose and a spiritual purpose. I can't tell you. Only you can find out what it is."

"I've been looking for the truth my whole life." Sky confessed. "I did not understand why you were taken away from me. Is our spiritual gift meant to make us crumble or strengthen us?

"I have not been taken away from you. I'm still in the flesh realm and I'm here in the heavenly realm too." her mother reminded. "In the bible God says he has plans to prosper you and not to harm you." Sky touched her mother's face and touched her beautiful long gray braids. Makeda reached into her basket and pulled out salt. She poured salt all over Sky's feet and said,

"You can't stay here too long. Your earthly body is left unattended."
Sky did not want to leave but she hugged her mother. "When you walk out of this place do not look back. Just walk straight out." her mother instructed.

Sky walked back down the path and fought the urge to look back at her mother, but she was obedient to what her mother said.

As she came to the entrance of the forest, she saw herself sleeping on the couch. She couldn't believe that she was out of body. She kept approaching herself and stared in amazement at herself. As soon as she touched her own eyes, she felt a suction and she woke up in what she learned was called the flesh realm.

Sky looked at herself in the mirror and wondered if she was dreaming. "I know that wasn't a dream," she said out loud. She touched her eyes, mouth, ears, teeth, and hair. She walked upstairs and punched Job into the search engine. She read the bible by herself for the first time in her life. Sky was filled with an overwhelming feeling that her mother was alive and close by. *The forest, the forest.* Sky thought to herself. Then it occurred to her. Franklin Park! Her mother literally showed her where she would be in the future when she was a little girl. The hospital in back of Franklin Park!! The forest was beginning to have multiple meanings.  Sky knew she had to visit the hospital.

## 15

## The Space Between Snow

The hospital was in the back of the park. It was secluded and emerged suddenly, disturbing the peace and beauty of The trees and their fall colors of greens, oranges, reds, and browns. The building was a twelve storey tall eye sore and looked like a red brick that had white windows drawn on it. Sky stood outside for a few minutes and observed a group of men in hospital robes. She waited for a text from Sharon to confirm that the visit was arranged. She hid behind her sunglasses as she passed the group. She checked in at the front desk and waited for the receptionist to call her. They escorted Sky onto the elevator and then to a room where they checked her purse and body.

She was then escorted down another hall to a locked unit. She heard voices, banging, and people calling to her as she walked to another room.  She waited in the visiting area for what seemed like an eternity. The facility was so old and outdated it reminded her of some of the places she was held as a child. Cinder blocks walls painted green and cold floor. The room made her feel cold.

They wheeled her mother into the room. She was tied in straps to the wheelchair. She was lethargic. The nurse raised her voice. "Makeda! Your daughter is here to see you!" Makeda stared straight forward. Sky could hardly swallow and suddenly did not know where to place her hands or even where to sit. "It's her medication that keeps her calm," the nurse told her. Sky found the courage to sit next to her mother. The nurse continued "The visit will only be thirty minutes as recommended by her doctor because Makeda is combative when her meds start to wear off."

Sky was annoyed but did not have the strength to advocate for more time given her current wave of emotions. Her mother's skin looked dry, her hair was uncombed, and she seemed to not know she was even there. Sky managed to sit next to her mother and hug her. She placed her hand into her mother's hand and cried. The longer Sky sat there Makeda's hand started twitching. She felt her hand twitch in hers. "I'll be right back," the nurse barked as she left the room.

Sky could hear the nurse outside, flirting with the security guard. Sky knew she was over the time that was quoted to her by the nurse. Sky began to sing the song her mother used to sing to her when she was a child. "Tell Mommy all about it, tell Mommy about it, tell Mommy all about it, tell Mommy all about it, tell Mommy all about it, tell Mommy all about it!" She felt her mother hold her hand back in response as if her mother seemed to thaw.

The nurse abruptly entered back into the room and announced, "Ok it's time."

Sky left the hospital full of guilt. She had not seen her mother in ten years. She was so busy surviving and thriving she didn't even bother to check on her own mother. Anger from being abandoned blinded her. Unforgiveness and hate allowed her mother to be in that state. She realized that her mother's life was just as hard as hers.

At home, Sky's thoughts would not let her rest. Her mind was on Preston, the visions, Solace and Love, The

Maker's House, and Marlon. Her mind was racing between the past and the present. Angry for accepting trinkets of love in exchange of keeping quiet, getting used sexually, when needing love so bad. Being left empty without a companion. Holding onto memories to stuff down the real emotions or the real discussions. She cried and screamed at the top of her lungs. She was a villain. She was a victim simultaneously, but at that moment she decided to be a victor.

The next day Sky returned to the hospital.

"I'm here to See Makeda Jones." Sky told the receptionist at the front desk. The receptionist typed in the name.

"She has been moved to a more secure unit and she can't be visited at this time." The woman responded.

"What? I just saw her yesterday." Sky said with surprise in her tone.

"Yes, she had an outburst when you left and had to be moved." the woman confirmed.

"An outburst? Sky questioned. "She was so lethargic. She couldn't even move."

"That is the information I have here." The woman confirmed.

"I'm sorry. I need to speak to someone else." Sky concluded.

The woman asked, "Sure, to whom would you like to speak?"

"Someone other than you!" Sky retorted sarcastically.

The hospital administrator came to speak to Sky.

"Why can't I see my mother?" Sky asked.

The administrator confirmed. "She can't have any visitors at this time."

"I'm her daughter." Sky emphasized. As the words were even strange to her.

"I'm sorry. I've worked here for five years, and I've never seen you visit your mother before." The administrator said, and stared at Sky with a smug half smile.

"That's irrelevant! Sky stated with annoyance in her voice. Sky continued, " I'm talking about today. Right now. I would like you to give me a valid reason why I can't see my mother."

The administrator firmly stated. "It's a safety issue. And given the situation, you have to get permission from her doctor, guardian, or court order."

"A court order to see my own mother?" Sky asked.

"Yes." The administrator responded firmly.

"Well, who is her doctor?" Sky inquired.

"Dr. Malcam," The administrator asserted.

"Abishai Malcam?"Sky asked with surprise in her tone.

"Yes." The administrator confirmed.

The name smacked Sky in the face, punched her in the stomach, and started to choke her. Dr. Malcam evaluated her as a child and was the resident psychiatrist at the Maker's House. Sky felt sweat come out of her pores and the hair on her arms stood up. She had known Dr. Malcam for most of her life.

"I'll be back." Sky reassured.

Sky gathered her anger and left immediately. Then, she called Sharon.

"Can you get me an emergency appointment with a family court judge?" Sky asked Sharon.

Sharon said, "I'm on it! I'll see what I can do."

Sky exited the hospital and paced back and forth with her new information. She wondered if Dr. Malcam knew she had been there to see her mother. She connected the dots Dr. Malcam, the Maker's House, and her mother. *Is he trying to keep me away from my mother?* She came to the conclusion. *He must know that she is my mother. How long has he been my mother's doctor and never mentioned to me that my mother was under his care?* She had seen him in staff meetings at least every two weeks for years.

Her stomach was twisting into knots and her head was spinning. Her heart was filled with sand and rocks at the same time. Those were familiar feelings she got as a child.

She hesitated for a moment, sat in the car, checked her phone, and saw she had twelve missed calls. She scanned the numbers to see who called then quickly, without thinking about it any further, called Solace.

She was surprised when Solace answered on the first ring.

"Talk to me." Solace answered.

"It's Sky." she stated.

"I know who this is. I know your voice. What's up?" Solace asked.

Sky said with urgency. "I need to see you."

"I'm at the shop on Norfolk Street. You can come and pick me up." Solace confirmed.

Sky drove from Franklin Park, continued down Blue Hill Ave, turned left onto Talbot, and ended up on Norfolk Street.

Her mind raced as if she were trying to put a broken glass back together. She pulled in front of the store and Solace was already outside. Solace jumped in the front seat. Sky was already crying.

"Talk to me," Solace said with a concerned face.

Sky started to tell Solace. "I saw my mother yesterday and when I went back to see her today, they wouldn't let me see her. I know something is not right. The crazy thing is that she was all drugged up and couldn't move. The longer I stayed there she started to move. Her fingers then her hand and her face. She actually started to hold my hand. I said to myself something is not right about this. They said my mother is violent when she's not on meds. Today I went back and they wouldn't let me see her.

I needed permission from the court or her doctor. You'll never believe who her doctor is."

"Who?" Solace asked.

"Dr. Abishai Malcam! He's been on my staff for years treating kids at the Maker's House. I trusted him because he treated me when I was a kid. I feel like throwing up in my mouth. I can't believe this. He's been looking in my face all these years and he knew my mother was in this fucking place and didn't say shit to me."Sky said with anger.

"Wow! The question is why?" Solace responded.

Solace was trying to pull information from the atmosphere, but she received nothing. The only time nothing happened is when she was around another prophet that was being spoken to at that time. The spiritual world was trying to speak directly to Sky. She looked at Sky and knew Sky must be a prophet. Sky was able to receive information from the spiritual world too.

Solace told Sky, "Sky, there are a lot of people that have a history with someone. They love that person for one reason or another. Some people are caught in a love triangle, cheating, or cannot get over an ex-boyfriend or girlfriend. They are in love with someone that they can't have but the reasons why it is happening to those people stay hidden. What is happening to you happens to people every day, but they are unaware that it is happening. The revelation of these things that are happening to you do not happen to everyone. The spiritual world doesn't start coming over or exposing itself in this realm unless you have access to the spiritual realm. The spiritual realm stays invisible."

"What do you mean?" Sky asked.

"You have a gift like right now as I am around you, I cannot receive information that means you have access to the information. I first started hearing things when I was a little girl. People thought I had a learning disability. I realized I couldn't wear things from thrift stores because I could hear things and see things about people. I cannot touch everything and everybody. You have to find out how your gift works. We need to go to the Makers House.  Do you have access to the house?" Solace asked.

"Yes, I do now" Sky confirmed.

"We need to go to the Maker's House. Are there any cameras?" Solace asked.

"Yes, cameras are everywhere." Sky responded.

Solace emphasized her question.

"Can we get them turned off? Someone is watching you Sky. You can't let them know what you know."

Before they pulled up to The Makers House, Sky disabled the cameras and the alarm system. Solace pulled out the oil and rubbed it on Sky's forehead, heart, palms, and did the same thing to herself. Solace grabbed Sky's hand and said a prayer in silence. Solace then said. "Ok, let's go!"

The building was pitch black as they entered.

They walked to where Preston died. Solace reached for Sky's hand as they both stood in the doorway and scanned the room. There were leftover traces of a police investigation. There were moved items and leftover coffee cups.

Solace prompted Sky to keep moving toward Dr. Malcam's office. Sky unlocked his door and turned on his light. A sweet aroma hit Sky and Solace. The office was extremely neat, and they both scanned the office. They walked around the room and Sky went to his file cabinet but realized her key to his cabinet did not work. They both walked around the room looking at all of the items. Sky gravitated to the stump of wood on the bookshelf and icy chills ran up her spine. The closer she got the more it pulled her. Solace on the other hand felt nothing for the first time in years.

"Let it happen," Solace encouraged.

Sky could not believe what she was seeing. The closer she got to the wood she started seeing the faces of the kids. She saw her daughter first and got scared and stepped back. She tried to shake it off.

"Oh my God, I can see the face of my baby girl that I lost. I really wanted to be her mother." Sky said remorsefully.  Tears started to fall on Sky's shirt.

Solace rubbed her back, "Don't be scared," Solace reassured.

Sky stepped forward again. She saw her daughter, Preston, another little girl, and two more boys. Do you think Dr. Malcam has something to do with Preston's death? She asked Solace.

"What does your instinct tell you?" Solace asked.

Sky knew he did but did not want to believe it. Then she saw Paris and stepped back.

"Why would I be seeing her?" Sky asked.

"See who? Tell me," Solace said.

"I saw Marlon's girlfriend when she was younger." Sky confirmed.

"Keep going." Solace encouraged.

Sky stepped closer to the wood again. She saw countless children. She stepped back again when she saw Marlon when he was a boy.

"I see Marlon! Why? Why am I seeing all of these kids?" Sky asked.

Solace looked at Sky and said. "You are getting closer and closer to the truth. Now we know you can see kids. We can find out what really happened to your baby girl, Preston, and all of the kids. Focus!"

"I'm not sure what we have," Sky replied.

"Close your eyes and step close to the wood again"

Sky closed her eyes and this time it felt like she was stepping into warm water. Solace placed her hand on Sky's back and started praying.

"I see more. This is bad!" Sky said nervously.

"don't be scared, lean into the vision, stop talking and see," Solace said firmly.  White flashes of different events began to present themselves. Sky saw various kids from the Maker's House in therapy sessions being taught Binka principles. She then saw Preston Johnson talking to

Abishai Malcam. The doctor convinced him to sacrifice himself. She then saw Dr. Malcam stitching fabrics together from Marlon and herself, and he mixed blood and hair from Paris and Pharaoh and poured it on the fabric from herself and Marlon.  She saw Kern with their daughter with Dr. Malcam. She saw the doctor slice and dismember babies. At that point, she could no longer take the vision. She stepped back from the wooden figure.

"Are you ok?" Solace asked.

"No!" Sky confessed with an expression of shock on her face.

Solace put anointing oil on Sky and asked "what did you see?"

"He murdered children." Sky said in disbelief.

"Suffer not a witch to live!" Solace said.

"What?" Sky questioned.

"That's a scripture from the bible" Solace confirmed. "it says, 'Thou shalt not suffer a witch to live. Exodus 22:18'" Solace recited.

"What do I do with all of this information? I can't go to the police and say I saw this in a vision." Sky conceded.

Solace reassured Sky. "Everything does not always get handled in the physical. You are definitely on a journey. The best thing is to pray and ask God for help. It will be handled trust me I know. You have to find God's will and get in it."

This troubles me. I have never asked God for anything after I was disappointed and I felt he did not hear me when I was a little girl. I know it's bad but it's the truth.

"God can handle your truth." Solace confirmed. "We got what we came for. Come on. We need to leave." Solace said with haste in her tone.

They exited being very sure to leave everything the way it was when they entered. In the car, Solace told Sky, "You have to find a way to get your mother out of that place."

"Indeed!" Sky agreed.

"You always talk about your mother. What about your father?" Solace asked.

Sky stared at Solace.

"I have no idea who he is, but that would be too much for one day." Sky said.

Solace busted out into laughter and Sky joined her.

## 16

## Gold Bowls of Prayer

"Bernadette here. I was wondering when you were going to call me! It's been a long time, my daughter. How can I help?"Bernadette playfully answered her phone.

Sky felt it was arrogant for Bernadette to assume help was the reason she was calling. She pictured her making the statement over her shoulder with her eyes slightly rolling the way she often spoke to people. Then sky remembered she was actually calling for help and calmed her flesh.

"I need help getting my mother out of the hospital." Sky found her voice trembling and her hand started shaking.

"I never heard you talk about your mother," Bernadette stated.

Sky responded, "I know. I'm trying to reconnect with her. I had one visit with her and now they are saying I am not authorized to see her, and that I need a court order. I went to court, and I am waiting on a date. Can you help me expedite the situation?"

"Yes, anything for you! I thought you were calling about what happened at the Maker's House. Do you need help with that too?"Bernadette asked.

"No, I am focused on seeing my mom right now. It is of the highest importance to me." Sky said as she imagined Bernadette on the other end of the phone in her mansion drinking wine with her pinky up.

Instead, Bernadette said, "Wow, I wish Kern would say that. He's doing him wherever he is. I will never forget what you did for my family." Sky heard tears and sniffles but did not know what to do.

"I was so excited about my granddaughter. We are family and you can call me anytime.  Even if you just want to grab lunch."Bernadette reminded Sky.

The loneliness in her voice was like a long empty hallway with marble floors that trapped sound and echoed through the phone. Sky imagined how much it must have taken for her to make that suggestion.  "Yes, I would like that." Sky affirmed.

"So nice of you to say that dear. Now let's get this situation sorted." Bernadette responded. As Bernadette asked questions about her mother's location, name, date of birth, and docket number, Sky drifted in and out of reality back and forth through time. Memories moved like she was driving in a car watching the scenery go by. The delivery, holding her baby girl with the brass skin, the baby that she named Blue. The staff forced her to give the baby. The funeral, the small casket, and the room where her and Bernadette cried. The marriage, the house, the family she wanted to forget.

Bernadette's voice was full of purpose. "Okay my dear, do not worry! We will get this situation SOR-TED out. I will be in touch"  Bernadette promised as she adjourned the call.

Sky was all alone in her apartment. She watched the light come in through the window and dust dance in the sun's spotlight. She could hear the air conditioner and the refrigerator buzzing softly in the background. Occasionally a neighbor outside would pass by on the other side of her front door. She breathed in and out slowly not knowing what was supposed to happen. Her mind zoomed from crushing loneliness to her mother and everything that had been happening.  She closed her eyes and when she opened them again, flies were everywhere. She smiled and did not swat.

She stood and slowly walked. The buzzing disappeared and then there was a place between sleep and awareness. A field was before her. Green grass beneath her feet and sure enough the woman was running. Sky did not hesitate. She ran beside the woman with all of her strength. The woman kept running towards the horizon. The woman and Sky's heartbeat felt like one. The woman jumped and spread her arms and legs wide apart, and Sky did the same. She felt warm air underneath her arms and heavy air pushing her up. Sky flapped her arms down and up again and warm air pushed her up. Sky saw the woman rising and she was rising too. Sky moved her arms up and down up and down. The woman looked at Sky and smiled and sharply turned right. Sky followed the warm sun beating on her feathers and her face. Rising and falling rising and falling. The sun gave her energy.

Sky examined her six wings. They were black and she could see all the colors of the rainbow. Sky's body was now blue like a peacock and eyes covered her whole body. The woman landed on the peak and smiled. Sky followed her into the place she saw before with the marble floors.

"Where are we going?"She asked the beautiful chocolate angel.

"We are going to see the Angel of death." The angel responded.

Sky was filled with fear.

She asked, "The Angel of death? How is death an Angel? I thought Angels were good?"

The angel responded, "Death is a part of life and no, not all Angels are good. Death is a good angel that has one of the hardest heavenly jobs."

Sky lost her fear the way one loses a loved one; gripping on reluctant to let go scared of the future. She was willing to face her fear though.

"What is this place?" Sky asked the angel.

"You are in the spirit. You are from the spirit of the fourth living creature that will initiate the worship of the elders at the end. The seven spirits of God are on the earth, and you have witnessed a great injustice and murder and perversion of innocent children. We are going to ask God for justice by entering a prayer in the bowl of prayers" The angel explained.

They walked in and there were twenty-four elders twelve on each side. "There are gold bowls of prayers that are sweet incense to our heavenly Father. He will hear them." The angels announced. Sky took her finger and wrote her prayer in the air, gold letters flowed out of her finger and the angel placed her prayer in the bowl. Sky was humbled and could not bow low enough just thinking about the glory of God and she began to cry.

The angel said, "After you petition God, If it is God's will,  the Angel of death would have to come to retrieve anyone who has died." Sky walked down the beautiful corridor and never saw so many flowers in her life. The hall seemed to have every flower from all of the funerals that have ever been since the beginning of time. Every butterfly, bee, and bug that passed away were working to keep the flowers alive. Water flowed on each side of the marble to the direction of the room. Her feet felt cold on the marble floor, but her heart was warmed by the sweet smells of prayers, sage, cinnamon, myrrh, and flowers.

At the end of the corridor, the room was open. A large black woman adorned in diamond armor paced back and forth deep in thought. As she walked closer, Sky's hands were shaking. The blue, orange, green, purple, and red sparkled and bounced on the wall and onto Sky's face. The clear glass iridescence of her armor seemed both liquid and solid. Her skin was the color of the deepest brown earth, almost black. She had two scars that ran from the bottom of her eye straight down to the bottom of her chin. At first, it looked like tribal scarring and then Sky realized they were tear trails that were carved into her skin from tears of mourning. Her long dreadlocks were full of gray. Sky's presence interrupted the angel's pace. Sky had never seen any garment like this before in her life. The angel of death had folded sparkling diamond rainbow wings. The angel of death opened her mouth, and the sweetest aroma filled the room. "kilak nome nome jubrona tatem baban ye shem laka lemen," she heard come from the angel's mouth.

Sky began, "I have come a long way to see you. I have already presented my prayer to God and I know this will all depend on God's will. I recently came to the knowledge of a man named Dr. Abishai Malcam. He has learned how to access a holding space in the spiritual realm so that when people die their physical body passes away, but their spirit is held in that place. He finds people that have the same love, bad habits, or brokenness and he releases the spirit of those who have passed before into the lives of the living. The people continue to perpetuate those same generational curses and continue to live out the will of the people who have already had their chance to live on the earth. In order to access this holding space, he has been paying the demon baby gnats in the blood of children that he sacrifices. The children are also in this realm unjustly and they cannot rest."

The angel of death said, "Heaven is already aware of these things. He was able to access this because whatever knowledge is in heaven is on earth and whatever spiritual knowledge that is acquired by the children on earth belongs to them. This is some of the knowledge from the tree they were instructed not to eat from. Jesus has also said that whatever works he was able to do man can also do. Jesus rose and some people have the knowledge. I can see that you placed your concern in the gold bowl of prayer so that our heavenly father has heard your heart and has agreed. There is only one thing." The Angel continued. "You must have clean hands. You yourself have to be washed in the Blood of the Lamb. You have to confess and triumph through your testimony. You have sinned but you are here to report the sin of another. God does not see one sin higher than the other so you must confess. You are who you are and you are where you are because you have lied, cheated, and finessed your way into your position. When you triumph through your own testimony and break the curse over you, you will break the chains off all Dr. Malcam's sacrifices of bone and blood. The demon and the spirits will no longer be fed by the blood of the children. They will no longer be held. They will be free. Once they are no longer fed, Dr. Malcam will owe a debt. He will not be able to appease the spirits and the demon. The Holy Spirit will seal him. He will no longer be able to come back to the earth and then I will confirm his death. The word of God says, Ecclesiastes 9 "Anyone who is among the living has hope. Even a live dog is better than a dead lion. For the living know that they will die but the dead know nothing; they have no further reward and even the memory of them is forgotten; their love, their hate, and their jealousy have long since vanished; never again will they have a part in anything that happens under the sun. Whatever your hand finds to do, do it with all your might, for in the grave where you are going, there is neither working nor planning nor knowledge nor wisdom. Here is what must happen. All people tied must be in the same place at the same time. Four elders with the knowledge must sit in prayer in this place. Somebody must plead the blood of Jesus to break the previous deal. A testimony of truth has to be made. the Holy Spirit has to be petitioned to come and I, the angel of death, will be present."

The Angel walked to the open area of the room and spread her wings wide. The wings extended the length of a city block. The blue, green, red, orange, and purple, light burst into the room. As the clouds floated, the angel prepared for flight. The angel descended and iridescent light was left in the room and what seemed like thousands of other angels followed, trailing behind her. Even Sky's wings moved when the Angel of death descended. Sky knew it was time for her to leave as well. The angel of the Lord that ushered her in stood beside her. They spread their wings and descended back down to the earth as well. Her thoughts were running wild. How is it possible for all of these things to happen as the angel of the Lord described? Sky asked herself.

## 17

## Wild Woman

Sky's mother came home on a chilly day in fall when the leaves were at their peak of color. God was in the wind that was blowing the trees outside. "SHHHHH, Shhhhhhhh, shhhhhhh." The sound resembled the ocean. In every direction, there was orange, yellow, light green, and maroon. Occasionally one leaf would fall slowly to the ground. The sun was the kind of yellow that made her mother's brown skin appear to have gold in it. Deep dark earth brown, black, and caramels mixed together. Her eyes were like cups of hot coffee and she had beautiful ivory teeth. Her matted hair and dingy-looking hospital robes could not dim her beauty. Sky and Solace wheeled her out of the dark hospital. She leaned to one side of the chair and drool ran down her face.

Sky struggled to get her into the car. Makeda stared straight and blinked slowly. Sky and Solace already agreed that they should all stay at the house with Solace and Love. Solace had the room prepared to receive Makeda. They carefully lifted her out of the wheelchair and into the tub of herbs. "Let her soak," Solace broke the silence. The tub was an old-fashioned round tub. Sky pulled up a chair behind Ma and combed out the matted braids.  Ma's braids were neglected and smelled like old milk and sweat. Sky watched the gray lint and black knots fall on the floor. Sky feared what was going to happen. She remembered the erratic behavior of her mother when she was younger.

She worked on her mother and tried to stop her mind from thinking.  She washed her skin, cleaned her nails, examined the old bandage and needle marks on her body, and washed her hair. She oiled her skin with Shea butter and re-braided her long hair into cornrows. Sky and Solace took turns checking on Makeda. She slept for two days as Sky and Solace decided not to give her any of the medication the hospital sent her home with. On the third day, she was sitting up when they went into her room. Sky approached her slowly. Her lip started Shaking as she attempted to talk. Solace walked in to support Sky, "Easy, take your time."

"I'm so thirsty." Makeda said.

Solace rushed out of the room to get some water. She returned and handed the bottle to Makeda and watched as Makeda devoured the water. After she finished drinking she sat up.

"Wow, you did it!" Makeda said to Sky and smiled. She was calm but she looked exhausted. Sky reached for Makeda's hand and Makeda reached back. Makeda motioned for Sky to lay beside her. Sky climbed in the bed with her mom and Makeda wrapped her arms around Sky. Sky cried silent tears at first and then burst into hysterical tears. They held each other and cried. "I've been in the wilderness for so long but now it is our time." You figured it out, I knew you would." Makeda said with joy.

"Are you hungry?" Sky asked.

"Yes." Makeda confirmed. Sky pushed the wheelchair back over to the bed.

"I actually do not need a wheelchair." Makeda shared.

"You can walk?" Sky asked.

"Slowly, but yes." Makeda announced. Solace and Sky were amazed to see Makeda walking on her own. They helped her down the stairs to the kitchen and they sat around the table to eat. Makeda slowly sipped her tea and rocked back and forth. Solace made herself busy making more toast and occasionally asked, "Do you want more butter? Do you need sugar?" in order to break up the silence.  Sky was silent. She looked at her mother when she thought her mother was not looking at her. She also looked around Sky and Love's beautiful house. The crown molding, beautiful colors, hardwood floors, plants, and beautiful furniture helped keep her eyes busy when she was not looking at her mother.

"We have work to do. We have to pray about Dr. Malcam. When he finds out I've been released, he will do everything in his power to hold on to what he has gained," Makeda stated.

"You mean to tell me this rude woman is your daughter." They heard Love's voice from behind them and Sky was annoyed.

"No way," Makeda belted out without even turning around. She recognized Love's voice. Makeda used the strength she had to slowly stand on her feet. Love rushed over and lifted her off the floor in an ancient embrace that surprised Solace as she had never seen her father, Love, show that level of affection for any woman.  Solace and Sky looked at each other and made eye signals of confusion.

Love's voice was full of softness. He said, "Solace told me they had you locked away in the hospital."

Makeda looked down and tears began to well up in her eyes.

"Yes, yes, yes," Makeda confirmed.

"Tonight is the night. All of us will pray and ask God to deal with Dr. Malcam." Love said with authority.

"I'm so sorry, we all tried to find you."Love empathetically said to Makeda.

Makeda and Love stared at each other with an intense longing that made the kitchen shrink. They looked into each other's eyes as if they were searching to find something that was lost. The language of people that share a secret. Makeda rubbed her hand up and down Love's arms and their closeness made Sky and Solace wonder about their acquaintance.

"Can we please have a moment?" Love requested. "I need to talk to Makeda."

Solace motioned for Sky to follow her to the back of the house. Sky followed Solace and they settled in a room that overlooked the garden in the backyard.  The beauty of the room made Sky's heart stop racing. The room was painted dark blue, and bookshelves lined two of the walls but instead of books, the shelves had jars filled with herbs, spices, liquids, ashes, and other colorful mysteries that Sky did not recognize. Solace led her to a couch with a table that had tea and cups already set and placed. Sky examined Solace. She could see the tattoo of 7:30 tattooed on her neck and quickly glanced at Solace's hair which was cut, curled, and layered to perfection. Her brown eyes and long lashes made her eyes look like a work of art.  She wore heels with her jeans and her earrings were almost down to her shoulders. Sky thought Solace looked out of place in the old-fashioned house.

"Those two seem to know each other very well," Solace said as she squinted her eyes. "Older people always have some business they're keeping from the rest of us!"

"Nothing surprises me these days with everything that has been happening." Sky acknowledged. "I have to tell you what happened at my house when one of the angels ushered me into the realm."

"There is no need. Just give me your hand. I will be able to see everything." Solace informed. Sky reached her hand out to Solace.

They held hands and closed their eyes. Solace was inundated with blue, green, red, purple, orange, yellow, and reds. She was able to see the elders, the gold bowls of prayers, and the Angel of death that lived with all the beautiful flowers. She was humbled by the experience, cried, and was more aware of what Sky had to do.

"Wow!" she said. The only thing now is for you to do what the Angel of the Lord said." Solace reinforced.

Sky twisted her mouth and said, "I do believe. I must find the courage and tell Marlon everything. I don't know what he's going to say. He's the only family that I have and he's the only other person that I love other than my mother and my daughter. I don't want to lose him."

"It's not just about Marlon. It's about confessing to God and forgiving yourself for everything that happened too." Sky encouraged.

Later, Sky and Solace were drinking their tea and talking about the realm. Makeda entered and Solace stood and gave her seat to Makeda. What were you two talking about?"

"We were just talking about Marlon." Solace answered.

"Who's Marlon?" Makeda asked.

"He's a big piece to this puzzle."Solace attested.

"He's my best friend and my family," Sky proclaimed."

Makeda tilted her head to the side, folded her arms, and said, "Why am I getting the feeling that there's more?"

"Sky was able to go into the heavenly realm and the angel of the Lord spoke to her about him. She has to make a choice." Solace confessed.

"Really?"Makeda said.

The room was filling up quickly. It seemed as if an elephant, clouds, smoke, and a big clown car was parked in the middle. Sky imagined herself in a flood with water rushing in from all directions. Sky wanted to retreat from the conversation, but she did not want Solace to stop helping her. Sky was also uncomfortable with Solace taking such liberties to tell Makeda so much information so quickly. Solace could feel that Sky was uncomfortable.

"Your mother is part of this process too. She's equipped and that's why she's here. She has been anointed to help you with this since you were born." Solace confirmed.

"Who is he again?" Makeda asked for clarification.

"He is my best friend." Sky responded with a guarded pitch.

Solace was glad that Ms. Makeda was asking these questions.

Sky felt ashamed. She knew her mother was only a few questions away from asking her what she needed to do about Marlon.

Solace interjected, "The angel of the Lord told her she has to tell him the truth and clean her hands through confession." Sky was uncomfortable because it seemed as though Makeda and Solace were gaining up on her. She felt like an outsider in her own situation as if they know something she does not. Sky tried to fight the emotions.

Makeda questioned, "Did you do something to him? What needs to be confessed?"

Sky twisted her mouth and bit the inside of her lip as she stared at Makeda.

"Take your time" Solace reassured as she could feel the tension building in the room.

"We have history. We were in love years ago and then we parted. We are best friends now and he's been there for me through everything." Sky attested.

"So, you said that you two used to be lovers. Why are you only friends? Did you try to get back together?" Her mother asked.

"No," Sky answered.

"Why not?"Makeda persisted.

"He's actually in a relationship with someone else." Sky said as she rapidly blinked her eyes.

Makeda's lips tightened. She closed her eyes and exclaimed, "I see."

Sky's mother looked at her with pity in her eyes. "He has a girlfriend," Makeda repeated with a hand over her chest. "Oh sweetheart, what are you doing to yourself? How does this work with you and him?"Makeda said with tears coming to her eyes.

Sky defended herself, "It is complicated. We are more than just friends. We are family."

"He's not yours though."Makeda replied as she let her tears flow.

Sky stared at her mother and could feel her tongue twisting in her mouth and gliding back and forth over her teeth. The sun made the dust in the air dance furiously and the air was harder to breathe. Sky crossed her arms.

*"Where the fuck was you?"* She screamed in her mind. She wouldn't dare say that out loud.  As she reminded herself her mom had just come home from the hospital.

*"God only knows what happened to her in there,"* Sky reminded herself.

"He's my family," Sky managed to say calmly through the anger that was rising.

"Does he consider you to be his family?" Makeda asked as she wiped her tears.

"I am pretty sure he does." Sky said confidently.

Sky wanted to yell, "Who the fuck do you think you

are?" Or, "Fuck you bitch!" Sky reminded herself that her mother may be crazy.

 "So, why can't you let him go if he has a girlfriend?" Makeda asked.

"You know it's easier said than done. It's nice that you want to talk about Marlon but what about us? You and I haven't seen each other in years. I think you want to focus on him so that you and I don't have to talk about us."Sky told her mother.

"We can talk about us too!" Makeda confirmed. Sky's emotions were out of control like a broken dam.

Sky walked up to Makeda and screamed. The kind of scream that you scream into a pillow, the kind of scream that leaves your throat sore. She felt herself digging her pinky finger into the palm of her hand. She felt her heartbeat, beat, beat, beat, beat, beat, beat, beat, wild. She felt the heat rising in her body, burning off her refinement and home training. She could see the memories of the girl that was left by this woman. She could see the hot water from the tub they pushed her in. The shaved bald head, the first man that touched her.  She stared into her mother's wild eyes and walked back and forth with her balled-up fist and wanted to slap her. Makeda did not take her eyes off Sky. They stood face to face so close their foreheads and noses touched and they breathed on each other. Sky wanted to bite her face, kick, or spit.

Makeda said, "Give it to me. I'll take it."

Sky screamed, "They beat me and touched me and played games with my mind. I am not OK! I needed you!"

Her mother started crying, and she held her belly. "Ahhh!" Makeda yelled out and began to cry. Gasping. Instead of hitting her mother, Sky beat her own head, chest, and body. Makeda grabbed her hands to stop her from hitting herself. Blood was pulsing in her head. Sky could feel her heartbeat in her head. She kicked her legs and wrestled against her mother. Her mother hugged her until she calmed down.

Solace stood with one hand over her heart and the other over her mouth as tears fell from her eyes too. Sky could feel that she was ugly. Her eyes were swollen shut from the salt and tears. Her nostrils were blocked now from the tears and over an hour of crying. Her body was weak and sore from the self-inflicted blows. She felt arms around her with no intentions. No strings attached. That day was another ugly day like many she lived through.

Solace and Makeda took turns handing Sky a tissue and wiping her face.

"Can I help you now?  I'm sorry I could not be there for you. It was not my intention. I always tried to protect you until I was unable to protect you. I was taken away beyond my control. Now you know that there were other forces at work. Please, please, please forgive me. I did all I could. I did my best."

Sky squeezed her mother's hand. Sky's tears fell and soaked her shirt. She looked down and the shirt was not enough to soak up the wetness that was falling.

"Can I help you now?" Makeda begged.

"I'm scared of what that means or looks like. I don't trust anyone."  Sky confirmed.

"You have to trust God." Her mother offered.

"Ma, Where was God when I was a little girl? I was crushed like a grape by loneliness, hoping and daydreaming about a Savior and no one ever came. You did not come. God did not come. Nobody came. All I had was myself." Sky confided in Makeda.

"Jesus Wept," Makeda responded.

"What?" Sky asked.

Her mother repeated, "Jesus Wept! When we feel like God does not love us, God's spirit is troubled.  John 11:35 the shortest scripture in the Bible says, "Jesus Wept." I know God seems far away but God actually cares about what we go through and cries for us."

Sky could not imagine a God that let people suffer.

"All of this is a lot to take in." She said, Why would God allow us to suffer? " I am doing my best not to break."

"You must remember, there is also evil and the devil is an enemy that you cannot see.  But look at you now. You're having an experience with God. He's speaking to you. He's speaking to all of us.  These things that are happening to you cannot be denied." Her mother pointed out.

"I know, but I'm mad at God. My heart is broken." Sky announced.

"There are also evil forces at work here too. 1 Peter 5:8 says, 'Be alert and of sober mind. Your enemy the devil prowls around like a roaring lion looking for someone to devour.' He's been trying to get you since you were born, Sky. Please believe me." Makeda pleaded.

"Ma, I do believe what's happening. I'm just trying to hold on to my mind. All my life I have been trying to survive on my own. Now I'm being asked to trust in what I cannot see and open up to people that I don't even know. I'm being asked to do things that require faith. I don't know if I can do what I am being asked." Sky confessed.

"There was a man that had a son who was possessed by a demon and the man asked Jesus to heal his son, but his problem was that he did not have faith. The man asked Jesus to help his unbelief. Jesus said to the man

'Everything is possible for one who believes.' Immediately the boy's father exclaimed, 'I do believe; help me overcome my unbelief.' This is in Mark 9:23.
God can help you overcome your disbelief." Her mother offered.  Sky remembered her mother used to talk about God all the time when she was a little girl.

"Ma, I'm not a good person. I lied to Marlon when we were younger. I never told him I was pregnant with his child and that our baby died. I pretended like the baby was another man's child in exchange for that family's connections. They bought me. I sold myself. I lied to get a rapist set free and then I lost my daughter." Sky told her mother.

"I had a granddaughter?" Makeda asked.

"Yes, Ma." Sky said dejectedly.

"That's ok. There are no perfect people. Romans 3:23-24 says, 'For all have sinned and fall short of the glory of God.  And all are justified freely by his grace through the redemption that came by Christ Jesus.' Jesus paid all your debts!  All you have to do is believe in Jesus.
For God so loved the world that he gave his one and only son, that whoever believes in him shall not perish but have eternal life. John 3:6." Her mother told her.

Sky asked. "Ma, can you please just talk to me regularly? Whenever you talk, you use the Bible."

"Yes, you are my daughter and only child. Please let me help you carry this burden. Let me lay these scriptures on your heart. I have held them in my heart for years. These are scriptures of God, and they will heal you, trust me. These scriptures helped me when I was held captive. They are for you now. They are working already. The prayers I prayed over you years ago are now coming true. Tell me your doubts and I will tell you what the Lord says. I know it seems like a lot but please as a mother this is all I have to give you. If you can't trust me, trust the experience that you're having with God."

Sky confided, "When all of this started happening, I thought it was punishment, Karma, or payback for all the lies I told, and the things I had done. I also felt like I paid my debt already because I suffered as a kid."

"Know this, 'The Lord is compassionate and gracious, slow to anger, abounding in love. He does not treat us as our sins deserve or repay us according to our iniquities. As far as the east is from the west, so far has he removed our transgressions from us.  Psalm 103 says this," Makeda confirmed.

"Sky, when these thoughts come up in your mind, I want you to seek a scripture that stops you from making negative inner vows. You need hope to combat the bad things that we want to tell ourselves."  Makeda encouraged.

"Ma, I don't know the Bible as you do. I wouldn't even know where to fish out these scriptures you're talking about." Sky explained.

"We will help you," Makeda said as she reached for Sky and Solace and the three of them held hands.

"We will get you ready, so the Angel of the Lord can come down and the Holy Spirit can deal with Dr. Malcam," Solace agreed.

"I'm scared that I'm going to lose Marlon if I tell him the truth." Sky admitted.

Solace interjected, "You need to worry about losing you. If he loves you like you say he does, there is nothing that can remove the love for you, especially not the truth. The Bible says, in 1 John 4 that there is no fear in love. But perfect love drives out fear because fear has to do with punishment."

I hurt him real bad in the past and nothing is simple between Marlon and I." Makeda told her mother and Solace.

"The Angel of the Lord told you how to get free. The confession that you need to make is to God and then your testimony will set you free." Solace cut in.

"More importantly than Marlon, what about you? You have to love yourself." Her mother reminded her.

Sky shook her head no! Her voice was hoarse from yelling and screaming. "I don't know how to do that." Sky said transparently. "I thought loving myself meant putting myself first, protecting myself from pain, surviving, outsmarting, and dressing beautifully. All of that stuff is superficial." Sky realized.

"You are not just flesh, you are also spirit. What do you do for your spirit?" Makeda asked Sky. "The thoughts in your mind are not flesh. The love in your heart is not tangible. What makes the tears come out of your eyes? What do you do to love your thoughts and protect your heart? What do you feed your spirit? I want you to give yourself forgiveness. Forgiveness is the biggest gift and act of self-love you can give yourself. Even when or if everyone tells you that you're ugly inside, useless, or worthless. You have got to believe there is goodness in you."

"Ma, I'm not a good person." Sky emphatically confessed." Makeda cut in again. "So, you can become one. I refuse to believe that about you. I know there is goodness in you because look what you're doing for the kids. Repeat some good things about yourself every day even if you don't believe it." Makeda continued. "Say it until it becomes true. You have to be diligent about beating back all the lies and negative things that happened to you and that were said about you. The starting point is what you say out of your own mouth"

"We need to fast," Solace suggested.

"Yes," Makeda agreed.

"Do you want to fast?" Solace asked Sky.

"What is fasting? What exactly will we be doing?" Sky questioned.

"Fasting is abstaining from food or other things to hear from God," Solace confirmed.

"Fasting destroys yokes and bondage," Makeda added.

"What are yokes?" Sky asked.

"Things that have you tied or trapped. Fasting will equip us to do what we need to do. It's when you set yourself apart for God so that you can hear him clearly. It will lift the burdens off of you." Solace assured.

"Do you want to try?" Makeda asked, "We will be in it with you."

Sky looked down at her hands that were shaking and looked up again.

Makeda promised, "In that time, we will teach you the word."

"I'm not sure. I need to think about it." Sky said apprehensively. "In fact, I don't need to think about it anymore. It sounds like it really has to be in your heart. I want to be as honest as possible with myself. I am tired of pretending. I only want to do what's real. As a matter of fact, I'm ready to go home. Solace and Makeda shook their heads and agreed.

"Let us know if you change your mind." Solace reminded her.

Sky exited the room and walked up to her room, packed, and went home.

<u>17 ½</u>

Sky retired to her room early. She reflected on how emotional those past couple of days had already been. *"How can I doubt?"* she asked herself. *"Clearly God is real,"* she confirmed. All of the evidence she was experiencing firsthand confirmed that God was real. *"What is my problem?"* She asked herself. Counting these thoughts would not allow her to sleep. The night was not kind, for it was filled with tossing and turning.

Sky woke up at 3:30 a.m. and light was coming through the corner of the blinds from outside. She walked over to the dresser, and she looked at herself in the mirror and was able to see herself in the dim lit room. She covered her mouth quickly with two hands to stop the sound from escaping. She didn't want anyone to know she was weeping even though she was alone. She bent over to touch her toes to stop tears from falling. She had learned that trick as a little girl. Her knees bent and she ended up with her palms, knees, and the top of her feet on the ground.

She began to rock on all fours and began to speak. "Please help me! I see you work for other people, but it seems as if you have overlooked me. I don't know what I could have done to anger or upset you as a little girl. My life has been horrifying. If you are real to me, I need you to help me. I don't know what love is. I have never seen love." Sky pleaded. Sky stopped talking and asked herself, "What am I doing?" She turned around and sat on her bottom. She swallowed hard and sniffed. The room was silent. This is what usually happened when she called out to God. No response, no sound, nothing. The silence made her cry and feel lonely. She continued talking into silence and in the darkness of the room even though she felt stupid. "What do I even call you? I called you so many times!" Sky said. Her pleading was met with silence again! Sky's tears were falling more.

"Repent and confess, they say. Repent for what? Who is responsible for me being in this world? I am not buying this because I did not ask to be here. You were supposed to take care of me. I was a little soul." Sky said through her sobbing. "Do you hear me? I just want you to see me one time, hear me one time." Sky thought "Is this crazy? I am talking to myself! I tried to be quiet and smart and stay out of the way. They still shipped me off from home to home and beat me. Now, I am numb. My baby was innocent too. Why did she die? Do I have to admit my sins? I have never been shown kindness in my life. We are down here just trying to make it. You sit up there far away on the throne watching us fail. What kind of game is this?" Sky questioned.

"Now I am what I have experienced, and I am supposed to feel guilty and offer repentance and apology to the one that could have shown me mercy. Look at your creation. I am with another woman's man. I was so broken I let a man rape and brutalize me with my permission. I am so ashamed. Can you heal that?" Sky was now sobbing uncontrollably, waiting for morning to come. The room echoed back her own voice. Silence from the God she was talking to.

"You owe me an apology. You owe me an apology. You owe me an apology," Sky chanted to a silent room over and over again.

She rocked back and forth and for a moment thought she felt something and realized she was just comforting herself. She walked over to the mirror and her reflection yielded no comfort. *How was she this angry*, she thought to herself. Sky put on her long goose feather coat and boots. She ascended the stairs to the top of her apartment to the rooftop. The cold air greeted her. She watched the navy-blue skyline, and the roof was filled with dark light.

Smoke came out of her mouth, and she could feel the cold air enter her body. She felt her heart beating in her chest. She felt the cold on her nose. Birds began to fill the sky with morning exercise. The waves in the water before her moved up and down. The cold air around her skin was there but could not be seen. The sun began to rise to make her skin orange and warm. The birds started to move erratically and then in unison.

The wind blew against her hands and eyes. The half-naked trees in the park below tried to hold on to the last leaves. The air was alive. The birds, the water, and the trees were moving. The day was waking up. Pink started to drip into the sky as an orange began to climb and saturate the man-made bridge, which was nothing in comparison to the splendor of the birds and the water on the horizon. The beauty of it all created a sense of peace within.

At that moment she reached into her coat pocket and felt a small piece of paper. She pulled it out and unfolded the edges. She recognized Solace's handwriting. The paper read "And when he had given thanks, he brake it, and said, Take, eat: this is my body, which is broken for you: Do this in remembrance of me. 1 Corinthians 11:24

"Bullshit!" Sky rejected.

Sky immediately remembered this scripture used to be hung on a sign in Ms. Jessie's bathroom. Sky's brain fired rapidly as she thought about how Jesus was broken. everything was connecting at this moment.

Sky remembered when her life began to turn around for good the day she arrived at Miss Jessie's house. Miss Jessie gave her a key to the lock on the inside of her door so that she could control who was allowed to enter and exit her room. She felt safe for the first time in her life. The laughter that came back when Miss Jessie bought her dolls and clothes of her own. She remembered Miss Jessie praying for her.

Sky also remembered wandering off away from a family that was fostering her and being in the pool alone at Sturbridge village after hours. Sky stepped off into the deep end and remembered watching bubbles rise as she sank. She remembered waking up on the side of the pool wet and alive, unable to explain how she got out of the pool.

Sky remembered when she was in Italy with Marlon when the spirit she saw through the vortex was trying to harm her. Something behind her was protecting her. She knew it was the same protection that she felt when she was on the table laying on her back in the delivery room. She felt like she couldn't breathe and wanted to vomit and felt herself slipping away.  Then again when her daughter died and Sky stayed in the bed for three months crying and nobody knew about the pills she took to commit suicide. After she woke up something held on to her and whispered to her spirit and it gave her hope and strength to get out of bed.  What was this? This was with her now.

At this moment everything that Makeda and Solace told Sky about God was lining up with the experiences she was having now. Sky had the feeling of butterflies in her stomach. She was sober and stopped crying. Sky stood up straight at attention She observed the Sky full of birds, alas the Sky grew and the sun rose whatever was commanding the birds commanded her to stand. The current experience was nothing less than God trying to talk to her again. She never felt it before but today is when experience crossed the words that were being spoken to her from the Bible. I will never leave you or forsake you.

She recognized her own breath flowing in and out of her body and realized she did not have to command it to flow, it flowed automatically without her assistance. Her eyes blinked without her assistance and her heart pumped without her assistance. Sky was humbled by this experience. Her whole life she felt alone and now it was confirmed that she was never alone.

Jesus was broken for everything you have been through. Take communion if you remember what I did for you is the message that was being spoken directly to her spirit. The son, the father, and the holy spirit was real to her for the first time. Sky remembered and she asked out loud, "Father please save me, in the name of Jesus. I believe and I remember."

Sky was still, she was small, and she was large at the same time. Sky felt part of all creation. Made of the same things as the air surrounding her and the birds.

## 18

### Tectonic Shift

Sky filled a pot with water and put it on the back burner of the stove on high. Sky washed the peppers, tomatoes, and scallions, and placed them in front of the cutting board. "ZZZZZ, ZZZZZ, On my way soon," The text read. The music in the background was the only company to the thoughts in her mind. She took a deep breath and sat at the table and tried to calm herself. Peppers were first. The green and red pepper were diced into a finely chopped colorful medley.

Next, the garlic and onions were diced into the smallest squares ever. The scallions were added to the bowl as the flame under the pan warmed the olive oil. Sky lit incense and placed it on the wooden holder. The rising smoke reminded Sky to calm down as her stomach kept rising and falling. Sky dumped the garlic, onions, and scallions into the oil and the smell caressed and soothed her as she watched the medley dance.

After three minutes, she added fresh salmon with basil, sage, salt, pepper, Sazon, Adobo, garlic powder, onion powder, seasoning salt, dried mint, and a pinch of cinnamon. She let it cook for a moment and then folded the mountain of cooked vegetables into the salmon. She broke the tender salmon in the pan, breaking it until it married the vegetables and became a colorful blend of flavor and aroma. She added breadcrumbs and mixed the veggies, fish, and spices until they became the texture of cookie dough. The pot on the back burner was now furiously bubbling, so she dropped in the box of jumbo shells. She felt her pulse in her throat and tried to open her mouth for more air but the intake was restricted and even though she was breathing, it was hard for air to pass. Her mind was twirling in a million directions. She calmed herself and after about twenty minutes she pulled the pot off the back burner and drained the water to reveal the shells.

She started rolling the salmon mixture into balls and placing the meat into the shells. She placed the shells in a beautiful overlapping circle design. She paced back and forth and then put butter and thyme on low heat to simmer in a pan. She then added a seasoning cube, an alfredo sauce, and began to season the alfredo sauce. As soon as it started to bubble, she drizzled the alfredo sauce on the shells and added parmesan, mozzarella, sharp cheddar, and crackers on top.

The oven was hot and ready to bake the entrée. She put wine in the freezer and the cold air magnified the hot tears that stood on the rim of her eyes. She blinked rapidly so they would not fall.

She smelled salt when she breathed in through her nose from the tears she was fighting back. She wanted her face dry when Marlon arrived. Her chest was heavy and her heart was actually aching. Sky walked back and forth "deep breathe in deep breathe out," she said out loud"

Armed with knowledge. Dr. Malcam was her therapist, Marlon's, Pharoah's, Paris', and her mother's. She couldn't believe what she discovered. There were so many things she had to do. She had to become her mother's power of attorney and get her released. She had to tell Marlon the truth about their baby.

Sky knew what she had to do. The battle with herself was the biggest battle she had to fight.  This was not going to be easy.

She gestured with her hands and looked in the mirror to practice what order she was going to release information to Marlon.

"Skit, Skit!" Marlon yelled from the front door. Sky realized the chain was stopping his key from letting him in.

"Sorry, I have to keep things locked these days." She said as she let Marlon in. He stopped and looked her in the eyes. He pulled her into his body, hugged her, and all the tears she was holding back fell.

"It's ok, Skit, Skit." He said and sat on the steps next to the door, sat her on his lap, and wiped her tears. His warm spicy oil mixed with his smell was familiar and comforting.

"You've been through a lot but look at you, you're still standing." Marlon continued. Sky inhaled and felt his warm body next to her with his lips in her ear. She knew she had to get up. She stood and took his hand and led him to the kitchen.

"It smells great in here. Is that my favorite?" He asked her.

"You know it!" Sky said as she smiled and walked over to the oven with her gloves and took the pan out. The cheese was bubbling and the shells were covered with golden brown spots.

"I'm glad to finally catch up with you." Marlon stated. "Please tell me what's been going on with you. The news said the investigation is over and there was no foul play."

Sky placed the hot pan on the cooling rack in the middle of the table and got the wine out of the freezer.

"Yes, that's right. They didn't find foul play but there was foul play." She confirmed.

"Wow, was there some kind of cover-up?" Marlon asked.

"No and yes." Sky responded.

"What do you mean?" He asked curiously.

Sky sat down across from Marlon. He instinctively stood and started to open the bottle of wine and poured Sky a glass and then a glass for himself.

"Since this whole thing started with Preston, strange, unexplainable things started to happen to me." Sky explained.

"I know you started to tell me before." Marlon recalled. Sky lifted the shells out of the pan and placed them on Marlon's plate. "I thought something was wrong with me, as if I was going crazy like my mom did when she was my age." Sky continued. Marlon stared into her eyes with an intense listening gaze.

"I found out that my mom is not mentally ill." Sky confirmed.

"What?" Marlon questioned with a surprised tone.

"Yeah, she was wrongfully institutionalized." Sky replied.

"Wait, wait, wait, wait! Back up? You saw your mom?" Marlon asked with a puzzled expression on his face.

"Ok, I'll back up. The story goes back further than that." Sky explained.

"I'm listening," Marlon said as he leaned in.

"Remember when we were in Rome?" Sky asked Marlon.

"Yes, how can I forget?" Marlon answered as if the response was obvious.

"Remember you found me naked at the Villa Borghese at night." Sky recalled.

"Yes." Marlon said with anxious energy in his tone.

"I was scared that I saw a man and some kind of spiritual vortex opened in my room." Sky reminded.

"Yes, I remember," Marlon said as he started eating.

"I found out why that happened and also what happened to Preston, my mother, you, and I." Sky explained apprehensively.

"So, what happened?" Marlon asked, trying to move Sky's explanation along.

"Please try to keep an open mind when I tell you these things." Sky said.

"Come on now, you're talking to me." Marlon said.

"I know but this stuff is far out there." Sky admitted.

Marlon picked up his glass, drank all of its content and joked, "Well I better get some more of this in me!"

Sky stopped to think as her saliva glands filled with water and demanded to be swallowed more and more frequently.

"I'll tell you what, you're not the only one that has had strange things happen." Sky was relieved by Marlon's interjection. She sipped her wine and took a bite of her food as Marlon recalled. "A couple of weeks ago, I went to my parents' house and dreamed I was drowning. It felt so real. Some woman that I have never seen was clinging to me for dear life. It felt so real." Marlon stressed.

"Oh my God," Sky said.

"So, what happened?" Marlon said as he pressed her to continue her story.

Sky began, "I was seeing this woman that I didn't know running past me and I could feel all of her fear and anxiety each time she passed me. My office would disappear, the coffee shop would disappear, and it didn't matter. Sharon told me a couple of years ago she had a problem that couldn't be fixed. She said she had a spiritual problem. I went to see these people and they were asking me a whole bunch of personal questions."

"I know you weren't having that!" Marlon said and laughed as he filled his plate with more food and his glass with more wine.

"I sure wasn't. I left that place and the visions got more intense and started happening anywhere and everywhere even when I was driving. I went back to the people and the father refused to help me and things were really spiraling. One day I saw his daughter again and begged her to help me. She agreed and then she told me about four people that were trapped in a love triangle in the past. A man and a woman were lovers that were torn apart. He ended up marrying someone else and fell in love with the woman he married. His first lover became jealous and went to see a spiritual authority. A spiritual deal was made for the first woman to have the man forever, and a baby was killed to seal the deal.

The husband and the wife were sold into slavery and ended up drowning and that is why your dream is fascinating to me. The man who made the deal is called a Shifter or Binder and he holds these people in a spiritual place and when he finds other people who have the same set of spiritual particles, he can release those spirits to live out their love story again, and again. They are soul-tied. Soul ties are made through blood and spirit agreements. Parents to children, sex, or any interaction where blood is exchanged. The other people die in the flesh, but the binder knows how to reincarnate himself and he dies and comes again, again, and again. I found out who the binder is because I am also a binder.

"Sky, this is a lot!" Marlon responded. "But I want to believe what you are saying is true."

"Marlon, I don't know how to say this but my mother, Paris, Pharaoh, you, and I have all been treated by the same therapist." Sky revealed.

"I know him?" Marlon asked.

"Yes!" Sky confirmed.

"Who? Dr. Malcam?" Marlon asked.

"Yes," Sky confirmed.

"Yes, I know him and the African man." Marlon confirmed. I used to see the African man in my sleep. That's why I was admitted into Abishai's facility. I couldn't stop seeing him." Marlon sat in shock. Sky's lips moved and the words she spoke validated his story. He was not crazy.

"Did he give you medication?" Sky asked.

"No, I did blood therapy with Paris." Marlon confided.

Sky continued. "He's been playing a game with all of us. He linked us all with familiar spirits. and we have unknowingly helped him feed demons.

Marlon interrupted, "Sky, that's too much." I don't even want to think about going back to that mental place again, where my mind felt like scrambled eggs and I couldn't tell the difference between what was real and what was fake.

"You're participating in it anyway." Sky firmly suggested.

"What do you mean?" Marlon questioned.
"You and I are going on as we do, it is not by coincidence, it's been orchestrated. He uses us to fulfill a blood deal he made with the people in your visions and my visions." Sky explained.

Do you want to be with me? I need more from you. We can't go on this way anymore.  Are you asking me to leave her?

"Yes," Sky admitted.

"I love you, Sky but I can't." Marlon stated firmly.

"You love me?" Sky asked.

"Yes, but I can't leave her. She is the one for me." Marlon professed.

Sky felt her blood boiling as she tried to calm herself down. Her blood was getting hotter and hotter and she knew she was not in control of what to say.  She tried to remember a scripture her mother gave her about the tongue or the mouth, but it escaped her at this moment.

"If you don't know me, then nobody does! It's like all these years no matter how good of a person I try to be to you it doesn't matter because of one moment that she was there for you. What about all the other times?" Sky asked.

"That one mattered the most." Marlon admitted.

Sky yelled, "I'm the one for you! You come over here and fuck me and extract all my emotions as punishment for what happened between us. You never got over it." Marlon was surprised and even though he has not heard Sky yell in years.

"There she goes, this is the one that I was waiting for angry Sky."  Marlon taunted.

"I won't leave her. Do you know what she has done for me?" He asked.

Marlon pounded his chest and pointed his finger into his skull.

He yelled, "I snapped! when you left me. I FUCKING SNAPPED! I couldn't hold myself together for years! I was unhappy in Italy when I was supposed to be living my dreams. I went to therapy, I was on medication, and I held everything inside because that is what I was taught to do. I was in love with you Sky. I still love you, but I chose her because she was there for me!"

"I needed to be somebody else and you did not save me. You didn't fight, you didn't let me know that what I would give up was worth what I was getting. I wanted you to tell me not to marry him." Sky pleaded.

"Fuck you! you're selfish, I loved you and you knew it. You made a choice to be with that asshole. Why am I the blame for that? Why are you coming now with all of this?" Marlon asked as he walked back and forth.

"That's why you chose her because she was there?" Sky asked again.

"That's right!" Marlon clarified.

"That's you, always seeing things from your perspective. I was supposed to drop my dreams and ambitions and follow you? Did it ever cross your mind that I had a right to live my dreams just as much as you did? I had more on the line. I had no mother or father and I wasn't born with a silver spoon in my mouth. I didn't have a support system. I had you and my dreams that's it. I wanted to be a lawyer. I had things I wanted to do. I did not have a safety net! If she's the one for you. Why are you fucking me?" Sky yelled.

"Do you think you're innocent? Your fucking me too! You know I have a woman.  You're the only one who gets me this way. Stop playing the victim." Marlon yelled.

"How? make you raw? Make you feel?" Sky asked.

"I'm over it."

"You can't even tell me the truth.  You came up with all this shit to tell me about witches and goblins and spirits. Be real Sky!" Marlon demanded.

"You want me to be real?" Sky paused before continuing. " In college, I was pregnant with our baby and I was scared as hell! Sky confessed.

"You were pregnant with my baby?" Marlon asked.

Marlon froze. He felt like someone walked through him. He felt his flesh melt off and then someone rinsed him off with hot water. He felt cold and his breath was shallow and all the air left his body. His mouth started salivating like he wanted to throw up.  He stopped in his tracks.

"What happened to our baby?" He said slowly.

"I gave birth but she passed away." Sky said and started to cry.

Marlon mouthed the words, "passed away?" silently as if he could not believe what he was hearing.

"The baby you had after you married Kern was my baby? Marlon asked.

"Yes." Sky confessed.

"What did you name her?" he asked.

Sky did not answer right away and Marlon asked the question again with his teeth clenched this time with tears welling up in his eyes and his jaw tightening. "What did you name her?"

"Lalibela." Sky revealed.

"Hmph, that's the name we always talked about naming our daughter." He reminded.

She tried to hold his hand but he moved out of her reach. "Who did she look like?" He asked.

"She looked like you, her eyes were big and she was beautiful brown with a full head of hair. She was a good baby, quiet, and didn't even cry." Sky recollected.

"What happened to our daughter? How did she pass?" He asked.

Sky started to cry more remembering the beautiful baby made out of love with the curly afro and the dimples. When she was two months old. It was said that she had Sudden infant death. Sky could feel herself getting numb all over remembering the baby's smell and gentle cry.

"You didn't give me a chance to see my daughter?" Marlon said bitterly.

"You were in Italy and I didn't know how to tell you, I didn't want to be rejected by you again." Sky offered.

"That would not have mattered! I would have done anything for you and our baby." Marlon yelled.

"But you didn't though!" Sky said confidently. "It would have required you to put us first and stay in Boston."

"You are so whack and dark inside and lame. You suck the air out of every living thing. I thought that maneater was just a term I used to hear men throw around but you are the definition in the flesh." Marlon said with all the venom he could find.

Sky interrupted. "You want to say these things to me, but you take no responsibility for who you are. You have no self awareness. You have no self mastery. I am supposed to be so dark but you attracted me to you. You're in a relationship with someone else and you keep running to my bed. I'm trying to tell you because I'm trying to be a better person."

"Be a better person? Twenty years? Twenty years! You kept this to yourself? You used my baby to get into a family and put you in your position. You didn't earn your position. You say I was born with a silver spoon in my mouth. You paid for your spoon with pussy. You want to tell me about some evil doctor. The two of you are the same person.  At least he does his shit in the open. Yours is in the heart." Marlon said as he clasped his hands.

"Yeah, you were taking things from a dead woman! I was dead inside. letting you fuck me over and over again with no commitment. Lying to myself just for you to see me, because I always wanted a family." Sky admitted.

"I loved you and I couldn't let you go but what you just told me is the last straw." Marlon said as he began gathering his belongings.

Sky had to hold on to the kitchen chair. She slowly blew air out but found it hard to pull it back in. She felt hungry and at that moment she knew that there was no more life between her and Marlon. All the time they spent together he thought she was a monster. All of her ugly scars were exposed and he hated every one of them. It was in direct contrast to the love he had for the one he chose. The woman who was equally imperfect to Sky. Her chest, her head, hurt. There was no forgiveness for her. The thing that hurt the most is that Marlon could not see her heart and the love she had for him. He could not see her fear of telling him made her lie. But she was free from this now. All the hours of bed confessions did not add up to true love. And at that moment she wanted to scratch his eyes out for not seeing her understanding. There was no forgiveness, not one sign of empathy. Sky knew that there were people who have done more than that and they were still loved. She saw that maybe he loved her before but not now.

Sky confirmed Marlon's sentiment.

"Today is the last day for us anyway. I always knew if I told you the truth you would run. I need someone who can see me at my darkest, my worst, and decide to love me anyway. Even murderers have people that love them, I deserve no less. Abandoning is not love. You say you love me but your love is light. It's not made out of much."

"Nah, I don't love you anymore." Marlon said coldly.

"You walked in the door and you loved me and two hours later, you don't. That's not love anyway. Your love for me is light, it's never been substantive. I thought you were good because of my guilt. You're not good."

After Marlon put his book into the briefcase, put his shoes on, he started removing the key to Sky's house from his key ring. When the key was finally freed from the ring Marlon said, "I don't want anything else to do with you anymore. Here's your key Sky. Goodbye."

Sky stood in the moment watching everything as if it was unfolding in slow motion. The first time in her life she found this profound desire to show up for herself to rescue herself and show herself the ultimate compassion and forgiveness and free pass. She did not feel abandoned or left behind.  She began to walk Marlon to the door and as she unlocked the door she said. "For the record. I am not some unwanted piece of trash." I want me!  Know that before you leave. Bye Marlon!" Sky said with absolute confidence.

<u>19</u>

## Seeking to Devour

All Staff,

Preston Johnson was an amazing, vibrant, smart child that resided at our facility. Unfortunately, the tragedy of his death happened on our campus. The District Attorney's office investigated this facility by conducting staff interviews, reviewing video surveillance, and performing a thorough investigation that cleared the Maker's House and all personnel in a no-fault decision. The death of Preston has impacted all of us, as our main priority is to protect and honor children on the highest level. In order to continue to serve children and families in this community, the Maker's House is reopening.

    In preparation to reopen, there will be retraining of safety protocols, and a review of our confidentiality and privacy policies. It will take time to grieve and move forward. The Maker's House would like to offer grief counseling to any staff member that is having difficulty and would like to utilize this service. All staff are expected to return to work on December 8, 2020.

    If you have any concerns about the process or require more coordination of your return; please do not hesitate to contact our human resources coordinator Patricia Cummings

    Upon returning to his office at the Maker's House Dr. Malcam was greeted by this letter from human resources. He could detect that the atmosphere in his office had been disturbed. Nothing was moved out of place, but the bottle he left on his mantle had turned yellow indicating cells other than his own entered his office. At first, he thought of the police or the office cleaners. He took the vial to his lab and burned the contents of the vial to reveal its owner. He combined the owner's information with Pharoah's blood as he had done a million times before. He was surprised to hear the squeal. The one the spirits warned him about had been in his office. He left his lab immediately and went home to his altar. He started by building a fire. The basement was hot causing him to sweat. He removed all his clothes. Between sips of vodka, he poured vial after vial after vial of blood on the altar. At first, he sat still aware of his breath. Then the effect of the vodka took over, relaxing his limbs and tongue, giving him the movements and the language to usher the spirits in.

The aroma of human blood mixed with the ancient words brought them down. Each one arrived very slowly to sit around the altar. He felt the presence of the one that he met when the deal was first made and then the greedy one, he feeds every week. The angry spirit of Tuma arrived. That was the spirit who felt she had been tricked by Dr. Malcam. She immediately twisted his joints and made them writhe with pain. He felt like his nerves were being pinched and she caused a sharp pain in his chest to intensify.

The two prisoner spirits that jumped off the ship that never agreed to this bondage were with her under lock and key. Finally, what seemed like twelve thousand flies entered the room and Dr. Malcam bowed to acknowledge the demon Baby Gnats. Upon the arrival of Baby Gnats, Dr. Malcam sliced his leg deeply and petitioned them. "Our agreement is old and ancient, but I will honor every word. I will continue to feed you all but there is one that knows about me. She has to die."

The spirit of Tuma angrily replied, "Do you know what it costs to cross over from spirit to flesh and physically touch a purchased child? Are you crazy? That is why YOU are in the earth realm so that you can hurt them. Do you want us to be dealt with by the Holy Spirit? Luke 21:16 says, 'You will be betrayed even by parents and brothers and relatives and friends, and some of you will be put to death. And you will be hated by everyone because of my name. Yet not even a hair of your head will perish. By patient endurance, you will gain your souls.' You have gotten beyond yourself. It is not our problem that you have been careless. I'll tell you what, you owe your debt or death."

Baby Gnats said, "She has petitioned heaven for help. You have to figure this out on your own. The only thing we can do is let you know where she is. Right now, we are unable to see her location. I have invested so much time feeding these people their fleshly desires and making sure they stay bound by blood and generational curses. I would hate to see my yokes undone. The greedy spirit chimed in. You feed US blood. It is not the other way around. I am hungry. I'm not interested in being fed weaknesses."

Dr. Malcam thought about what the spirits said. Then the thought came to him. *Sky is the most recognizable face in Dorchester and Roxbury right now. If the spirits can't see her then surely someone in the flesh knows where she is.* The doctor called all favors. He started with his congregation and allotted all the resources. He asked the mothers whom he loaned money to, the men who asked him to get rid of dead bodies with no questions, and he called politicians. He had people check stores, parks, and churches, and waited for her to return to work. Sky was nowhere to be found. He also put the word out to the most heinous. "If you see her, hurt her."

And then it happened. Dr. Malcam got the call. Sky returned to her home, and she was with Marlon. Dr. Malcam located the vial he had taken from Marlon all those years ago and called down the greedy spirit to listen in on what they were saying. He was frustrated when there were bird screams from the angels blocking him from listening. The spirit of Tuma appeared to him and told him to do something as something was happening to the connections that he promised. His promise was being broken. When Marlon left Sky's apartment, Tuma tormented the doctor all night. She ached his chest and bones. "You promised he was going to be mine forever." The doctor could not concentrate, for she caused him to sweat and shake and tremble.

Dr. Malcam finally got the call, when Sky exited her apartment after a sleepless night full of tears. She felt empty, drained, and weak. Her eyes and face were swollen. As she drove, she blinked only when her eyes started to dry out. She wanted the peace and refuge of the place she had lived in for the past forty days. She yearned for the songs and scriptures her mother lay on her and the friendship of Solace. She thought about Preston, the Makers House, and if she were ever going to see Marlon again. Perhaps her thoughts distracted her from the truck. Boom! Sky felt the glass fly in her face so hard and then the impact made her heart race. At first, she did not know what was happening, and then she heard metal bending. She saw her baby girl's face followed by her mother's face, solace, Marlon, as her car flipped and flipped and flipped. Then she saw green, blue, red, orange, pink, and purple as her car slid causing sparks to bounce on her skin and she smelled burning rubber. Then there was quiet. Sky was upside down and was not sure how badly she was hurt. She felt the pressure from the seat belt digging into her lap and collar bone. She heard other cars on the road screeching to a stop and she looked at the wheels drive by. She saw the footsteps from another driver approach her car. He knelt on his knees and looked inside. "Miss are you ok? Sky tried to speak but nothing came out. Something was stuck in her neck and her head was throbbing. The man reached inside and tried to free her from the seat belt. She heard sirens in the distance and blacked out.

When Sky opened her eyes, she felt sore all over. She felt cuts on her face. She could smell Solace in the room. The protection aroma was all over the room. Solace walked over to her and smiled. Sky tried to smile back.

"No broken bones, no serious injuries, no weapons!" Solace said. Rejoicing, she pulled out her phone and showed Sky a picture of her car. The car looked as if a giant stepped on it. The truck's impact was so bad the entire passenger side was pushed over to Sky's side and the frame snapped. The car looked like someone balled up a piece of aluminum foil.

Sky started to cry. "No weapon," she repeated. "Solace, I was hesitant about God. I didn't understand why a God would allow horrible things to happen if he was God. I was angry because I called on him a million times when I was a little girl suffering. Now I know that there is also evil. God has shown me firsthand. I felt his love for the first time. I had no idea that God speaks through circumstances or the people he places on your path. I think of all the times he saved me. I was special and I didn't even know it. I met you and my mother came back."

Solace poured oil on Sky's forehead. "I anoint you in the name of the Father, the Son, and the Holy Spirit. Lord, we ask for a hedge of protection and concealment from evil. May you prepare the woman of God to fulfill the purpose of your will, Lord."

"I agree, in the name of Jesus," Sky said.

Solace asked Sky "are you ready to fast now?

Yes, I am, he's trying to kill me.

"When we leave here, we are going back to the house where you will be protected. Your mother and Love are there. Miss Jessie's funeral is in two days.  "We will be ready," Solace proclaimed.

## 20

## Death of a Matriarch

The sun was bright and beautiful the day Ms. Jessie died. Paris usually had to fight 93 traffic but not that day. The call came. "Hurry please." She heard the crackle in Pharaoh's voice that she never heard before. She rushed from the salon in Chelsea to Dorchester in twelve minutes as if it were the weekend instead of rush hour. The clouds were like big fluffy pillows laying in the sky. Paris knew she moved fast as if two chariots were on both sides. She reached Lonsdale street. The porch was filled with faces she recognized who all looked at her as if they wanted to save her. Faces that read, 'Poor girl.'

Paris could not swallow. She ran past the living room on the right that was filled with somber kids and adults sitting on the couches and the floor, passed all the hundreds of pictures on the wall of countless foster kids, passed the desk, passed the plants, passed the cats to Ma's room near the back of the house on the right. Pharaoh's friend sat in a chair in front of the door. He stood automatically. Paris didn't say a word. He just moved out of the way. Paris entered the cool room where only Pharaoh and Ma's dog were.

Pharaoh's eyes looked puss-filled and puffy. He fell into her arms and trembled like he was cold. Snot ran down his face and when he tried to sniff nothing moved. He grabbed her hand and walked her over to Ma's bed.

"Ma, I'm here," Paris said with strain in her voice.

"Ma!" Pharaoh shouted. "Can you hear us? We're here, Ma!"

Ma's chest rose and fell, and Paris could see that she was struggling to breathe.

Paris fell to the side of the bed and her purse and keys hit the floor. She put her hands into Ma's hand and Pharaoh slid his hand into Ma's other hand. "Ma were right here!" He said again as his voice trailed off and crackled. Paris could not remember ever seeing Pharaoh cry. He grabbed Paris and Ma and hugged them both at the same time. Ma's chest rose and fell faster, and drool trailed down her face. Paris quickly wiped it and repositioned Ma's head. Paris felt her belly quivering followed by her eyes filling with hot water. Paris' tears made Pharaoh cry more. Tears drenched his white wife beater and wet his tattoos. The diamonds on his Cuban link were illuminated which made colors fire off like firecrackers. Paris and Pharaoh were on their knees, holding hands, holding Ma, with a puddle of tears gathering on the floor. The sunlight in the room disappeared as time passed and Pharaoh turned on the light. Paris looked like she had been in a fight.

Paris put her hands on Pharaoh's shoulders and looked into his eyes. She could hardly see his eyes because the lids were swollen shut.

"She's holding on for us!" Paris acknowledged.

Pharaoh squeezed her hand and said. "I know, I know!"

"She's holding on for us." Paris repeated.

Pharaoh pounded his hand into his fist. He shook his head no.

Paris squeezed his hands back and they walked back over to Ma.

"Pharaoh, I need you." Paris said. He laid his head back on the bed next to Paris. Paris moved her lips closer to Ma's ear.

"Ma we are here. It's me and Pharaoh and we are going to be ok. I'm going to love myself as you said." Paris whispered.

"Ma, I'm going to stay out of trouble. I'm going to make you proud." Pharaoh promised.

"It's ok Ma, you can go, you don't have to hold on for us," Paris said.

Pharaoh echoed, "You don't have to hold on for us."

"It's ok, Ma." Paris reassured.

Ma breathed in deep, deep, deep, and out and then no more breath came in or out. Paris couldn't believe what she was seeing. Paris couldn't believe Ma was waiting for their confirmation. She didn't expect her to depart after those words. She regretted the words immediately and wanted to take them back and rewind time. She felt like someone walked through her body. Pharaoh punched the wall with all his strength and wailed! Paris climbed in bed next to Ma, put her arm around her, and cried. Pharaoh climbed on the other side. They held onto Ma because they knew they had lost the only mother that ever loved them. Ma did anything for them with no hesitation and without any conditions. Just pure love.

They stayed that way for a couple of hours. Pharaoh and Paris had the hardest time when the coroner came in the small black van. They both held them up, for they didn't want Ma to be placed in a black bag. They couldn't wrap their heads around someone who gave so much light to the world sleeping in a cold dark place.

When the coroner drove Ma down the street, Pharaoh jogged next to the van until he couldn't keep up with them anymore. Most people were silent as Pharaoh and Paris floated like ships in mourning. Flowers and candles had already started to be placed on the porch as the community gathered.

Paris was showered with hugs from all directions from people she didn't know but knew Ma. As people tried to hug Pharaoh, he told them, "I don't want to be touched!" and walked back into Ma's room. Paris was in a daze. Everything seemed fake. The house was filled with strangers telling her words she couldn't hear.

When the congregation of Binka arrived, they came over with no less than fifty people. They were wearing dark red, and they all stood with hands behind their backs. Then Dr. Malcam arrived.

"Hi, Paris. Hi Pharaoh. I'm sorry for your loss." Dr. Malcam offered his condolences.

Pharaoh stared at Dr. Malcam with contempt. At one point he believed the doctor was good but after their history of disposing bodies, blood transfusions, abortions, plastic surgeries, selling organs, and other off the book medical procedures, he despised Dr. Malcam. Pharaoh was disgusted with the doctor but more disgusted with himself. He did not want to see him of all people right at that moment.

Dr. Malcam began, "We need access to her body for us to do what she would have wanted us to do."

Paris knew exactly what he meant. The doctor wanted her to be transferred to his funeral home so that he could retain a portion of her brain for the gods.

Pharaoh jumped in Dr. Malcam's face and interjected, "No fucking way! She's going to a regular mortician at a regular funeral home." One of the men in red jumped to his feet only to be halted by Dr. Malcam. Pharaoh lifted his shirt to reveal the black metal underneath his shirt.

"Why don't we all calm down," Dr. Malcam said calmly. We only want to do what Ms. Jessie would have wanted.

Paris wanted Dr. Malcam to officiate Ma's funeral at a Binka service in the temple of Moloch.

"I think this is what Ma wanted. This is what she believed at the end of her life." Paris pleaded with Pharaoh. Dr. Malcam put his arm around her shoulders and shook his head in agreement with Paris.

Pharoah walked over to Paris and motioned for her to go on the back porch with him.

Paris followed him and said, "I really think this is what Ma would have wanted."

Pharaoh insisted that she should be buried at a Christian church.

"I know Paris, but this guy creeps me out. Ma was baptized in the name of the Father, the Son, and the Holy Spirit when she was a little girl. She told me that she joined Binka only because it gave her answers. Paris, not all things are supposed to be for our knowledge. Sometimes we have to let God be in control."Pharaoh offered.

"She's not only a member but she's a priestess of Binka," Paris reminded him.

"Please trust me, Paris. I know what this guy does in his underground lab and temple and believe me, you don't want to commit Ma to him. She means too much to us.  You see how they all came over here trying to get us to decide on the spot in front of all these people. It's a manipulation tactic. Only the two of us should decide. They shouldn't be talking to us right now when we are crying and grieving and shit. Ma just passed. we can't even think straight but we must decide tonight? Let's at least wait twenty four hours." Pharaoh pleaded.

"You're right," Paris agreed. "What if we have the church officiate her service and Dr. Malcam can speak."

"That sounds better but let us go back out there unified and tell them we will not be deciding tonight." Pharaoh resolved.

Paris and Pharaoh were now in a time warp. The days seemed unreal. The days all merged until the day of the funeral.

## 21
## Communion

Ms. Jessie's house was quiet. "Shhhhhhhh, shhhhhhhhhh, Shhhhh, shhhh, the radiators hissed. Blong, Blong, blong blong blong blong the pipes clanged as the heat started to rise. Paris lay on her back listening to these sounds.  The sounds had changed throughout the night. Marlon's snoring, tires on the ground outside, the couple next door arguing on the porch. The room was now pale blue as light started to peek through the edge of the shades. Paris was tired but could not sleep. In this moment it felt as though the hottest tears she ever cried flowed down the side of her face and soaked into the scarf on her head.  She held her stomach and rubbed it in a circle the way Ma Jessie taught her to do when she felt empty.  Marlon lay beside her as she cried but she felt alone. She remembered Ma Jessie telling her, "you must learn to heal yourself!"  The flashes of Ma Jessie praying with her, teaching her how to cook, and saving her on the worst day of her life was front and center in her thoughts.  The clock read 6:12 and time seemed to be moving extremely slow and fast at the same time.  Paris showered and dressed in Silence. Marlon sat in silence and tried to be and do whatever Paris needed. He answered her phone screening calls from people wanting directions or asking questions about the service. He would straighten up after her and ask, "baby, are you ok?"  Paris would only shake her head yes with no words.

Pharaoh paced back and forth in the kitchen taking a sip followed by a puff.  He had Ma Jessie's pictures spread out on the table. He smiled looking at himself as a boy he must have been seven or eight. He was wearing his first pair of sneakers and his first video game was on the floor. Ma had her arms wrapped around him and he had his arms wrapped around her and they both were smiling. He never met anyone like Ma in his life. The woman that unselfishly helped so many. "What we gonna do now? Who's gonna help these kids?" he said out loud.  Pharaoh wanted to be finished with today and at the same time did not want to face today. His tears were continuously dancing on the rim of his eye.

Marlon watched Paris unzip their suitcase and put her shoes, dress, pants, panties, and bra on the bed. She examined three different outfits and was not sure what to wear.

        "It's going to be really cold out there today baby, why don't you wear this one?" Marlon suggested. Paris stared at him as if he did not say anything at all. He took the clothes from her hand and headed downstairs to iron her clothes.  Pharaoh was in the Kitchen, Marlon said, "Hey man, how's it going?

        "How you think it's going?" Pharaoh responded sarcastically.   Marlon tried to talk to Pharaoh more but only received short angry answers and decided to back off. He went back upstairs, and he watched Paris stare out the window. He helped her put her clothes on.    Marlon knew he was going to see Sky at Miss Jessie's funeral.  Everyone in the community was going to be there.  He thought about the baby girl he never met and how he and Paris were unable to have children of their own and it made him furious.  He had so many questions but stopped his thoughts in order to be present with Paris.  Marlon was relieved when Miss Jessie's other stepchildren and foster children started to arrive.

Pharaoh sat in the kitchen dressed and waiting for Paris to be ready. His phone rang. UNKNOWN caller appeared on the screen. Pharoah rejected the call. Again, an UNKNOWN caller appeared on his screen.  Again, UNKNOWN caller, he rejected it. Again UNKNOWN caller. He answered but did not say hello.

"Hello," Sky said from the other end,

" Hello," Pharaoh responded.

"Pharaoh, it's Sky!"

"It's been a long time, Sky!" Pharaoh confirmed.

"Indeed brother, too long!" Sky continued, "We lost all lost a piece of our heart"

"We sure did sis! Pharaoh agreed.

"Can I please say a few words at Ma Jessie's funeral?" Sky asked.

"What do you want to say?" Pharaoh asked.

"I actually would like to lead communion sky explained.

"Say more," Pharaoh encouraged.

Sky explained, "When Miss Jessie raised us she believed in the father, son, and the Holy Spirit and that's what she taught us. I know she was a part of Binka, but there's so much more at stake. It is important how we bury her. I don't know if you are aware of Dr. Malcam but he does horrible things with the bones and souls of people. We need to make sure his connection is broken off of Ma Jessie.  I know this all sounds strange bro, but you know how much I love Ma Jessie and I'm asking off of the strength that you know me as a sister ."

"This doesn't sound strange to me at all. This is confirmation of what I was already feeling about that dude?" Pharaoh confirmed. "Ok sis, you got that! I'll see you at the church."

"Thank you, thank you, thank you!" Sky said gratefully.

## 21 ½
## Communion Part 2

In Roxbury, at Solace's house, Sky cried as she remembered arriving at Miss Jessie's house when she was a little girl. She was greeted in the front by the other kids that hugged her. Miss Jessie's son Pharaoh took her black plastic bags up the stairs into a beautiful room with a pink canopy bed with white dressers. The room smelled like roses and it was so clean. Miss Jessie came into the room and she sat on the bed next to Sky and said, "you are welcomed here. If you need anything you can come and talk with me." Miss Jessie seemed old even back then. She helped Sky put her clothes into dressers and threw away those ugly trash bags. Sky stayed with Miss Jessie for two years until she was twelve years old. It was at Miss Jessie's house Sky had dolls, and friends, and learned how to swim and play double-dutch. Miss Jessie's house was the last time Sky remembered being a child. The Maker's House was an attempt to create what Miss Jessie was already to the community. Sky's heart was sad as she had to prepare herself for today.

Sky opened the door and started her ritual washing in the large bronze basin full of various spices and water. She got out, dried off, put on her panties, bra, and slip. She called Solace and her mother in for prayer. They had already begun the process. The oil was made with liquid myrrh, cinnamon, cane, and olive oil. Sky began anointing her face, stopping on her eyes and reciting scripture, careful and solemn the way her mother and Solace taught her. "The eye is the lamp of the body. If your eyes are good, your whole body will be full of light. But if your eyes are bad, your whole body will be full of darkness.  If then the light within you is darkness, how great is that darkness." She clapped her hands three times and Sky allowed Solace to turn her body to the left as she proceeded to anoint her ears, She said the next scripture a little louder than the first, "In my distress I called upon the Lord, Yes, I cried to my God; And from his temple he heard my voice, and my cry for help came into his ears." She clapped her hands three times and allowed Makeda to turn her body to the right. She closed her eyes and put both hands over her mouth. "Pray also for me, that whenever I speak, words may be given me so that I will fearlessly make known the mystery of the gospel." She placed one hand over her heart and the other over her stomach. "For our struggle is not against flesh and blood, but against the rulers, against the authorities, against the powers of this dark world, and against the spiritual forces of evil in the heavenly realms." She rubbed her hands together until they became warm and rubbed them up and down her legs. She finally stopped and her hands landed on her feet.  "And with your feet fitted with the readiness that comes from the gospel of peace." She made a full turn in the same spot and said the next scripture even louder, "Therefore put on the full armor of God, so that when the day of evil comes you may be able to stand your ground, and after you have done everything, to stand, stand firm then, with the belt of truth buckled around your waist, with the breastplate of righteousness in place, and with your feet fitted with the readiness that comes from the gospel of peace. In addition to all this, take up the shield of faith, with which you can extinguish all the flaming arrows of the evil one. Take the helmet of salvation and the sword of the spirit which is the word of God and pray in the Spirit on all occasions with all kinds of prayers and requests. Be alert and always keep praying for all the saints." Solace let the oil flow on Sky and her mother prayed for protection and petitioned the Lord for the Holy Spirit to come down. Her mother then began to wrap Sky's head.

Solace and Makeda picked up Sky's dress with a gold, blue, purple, red embroidery and put it on her. Lastly, she stated, "The secret things belong to the Lord our God, but the things revealed belong to us and our children forever, that we may follow all the words of this law." She closed her eyes and focused on her breath and soon she was no longer aware of her body. After they anointed her, she recited the scripture. "Verily, verily, I say unto you, he that believeth on me, the works that I do shall he do also and greater works than these shall he do; because I go unto my father. (John 14:12) Solace, Makeda, and Sky exited the room, and Love was waiting for them. "We are ready," Solace announced.

## 21 ¾
## Communion Part 3

Blue Hill Ave was lined with people that wanted to honor Ms. Jessie. It was unusually warm outside even though they predicted it would be cold. The people were standing on both the left and right sides. Some people placed their hands over their hearts, others clapped, some slightly bowed as the horse driven carriage with Miss Jessie's body drove by. They waved as the four limousines filled with Miss Jessie's children followed. The crowd started walking towards the church. The police had to accompany the procession as there were so many people in attendance. Paris and Pharaoh chose a beautiful white and gold dress to bury Ma Jessie in. Her casket was white with gold trim draped in beautiful flowers. Miss Jessie's head was wrapped in a beautiful silk scarf. Ma looked so peaceful. The first twenty rows of the church were reserved and filled with the children Ma Jessie fostered over the years.

Pharaoh and Paris were the last to arrive as they wanted to enter behind Ma Jessie. When they arrived at the church six service men stood in uniform completely still waiting to carry Ma in as if she were a soldier. The careful and methodical walk of the service men carrying Miss Jessie's casket created an atmosphere of solemnity, splendor, and honor. Pharaoh and Sky walked behind them holding each other's hands so tight it felt like they were floating and had no bodies. Paris and Pharaoh took their place in the front row and Pharaoh was relieved that Dr. Malcam was only a speaker and not the officiant.

The service began. Miss Jessie's children spoke of her kindness, service, and love. The people from the community wore lavender and gold as requested since they were Miss Jessie's favorite colors.  The choir rocked and sang in between speakers.  In the moment of loss, friends were able to share stories to soothe their grieving hearts, as they were able to laugh at some stories about Miss Jessie. In the things that were being expressed, there were also things that were not expressed. These things were unseen very similar to the breeze, radio waves, or electricity. The vibes, tension, worry, fear, heartache, and loss were unseen but very real.  There they were all in the same place at the same time. Marlon, Paris, Pharaoh, Solace, Love, Ms. Makeda, and Dr. Abishai Malcam. Every member of Binka in attendance wore red and as soon as Dr. Malcam approached the stage all seventy members of the Binka congregation stood. The color made their presence overwhelming and Pharaoh was annoyed that they would come so boldly and deflected attention away from Miss Jessie. Dr. Malcam approached the podium and scanned the room for Sky.  Sky was nowhere in sight.  Paris and Pharaoh sat in the front row. Marlon was in the row directly behind them.

"I have known Ms. Jessie for over twenty years," Dr. Malcam began. "She practiced Binka. In Binka, death is not a bad thing because we have equipped ourselves with full knowledge.  The full knowledge that enables us to overcome death.  Ms. Jessie knew this truth and she was able to help so many by providing a place of refuge. Her home was open to the motherless child. If she were here today, she would tell you not to cry but more importantly, she would tell you to believe in yourself and seek knowledge and open your eyes.  If you have knowledge there's nothing you can't do in this world. It empowers you." Knowledge is how Miss Jessie helped so many. All the answers and solutions to the mysteries of the world are within you. Jesus even confirmed it and the bible says the fear of God is the beginning of knowledge. Eve did not fear God until she ate from the fruit and gained knowledge. Don't weep because Ms. Jessie started to come into full and she ascended quickly in her lessons. Today we commit our sister to knowledge so that she may know in full what most of us know in part."

The Binka congregation clapped wildly in celebration and the others in attendance clapped because they were clapping. At 1:11 Sky entered the church and boldy made her way to the front of the sanctuary. Dr. Malcam saw her and felt as if ice water ran through his veins. He looked up into the balcony and saw the two elders Makeda and Love sitting together. Marlon, Paris, Pharaoh, and now Sky were all in the same place at the same time. Pharaoh saw Sky and Sky gestured to Pharaoh that she was ready to speak. It had been years since he saw Sky and he was delighted she came and decided that whatever Sky had to say about Ma Jessie was more important than whatever Dr. Malcam was saying. Pharaoh placed his body between Abishai and the microphone and stood in front of Dr. Malcam. Pharaoh interrupted,

"At this time, I would like to welcome another one of Ms. Jessie's daughters. Her stay at the house was brief but Ms. Jessie was so proud of her because she had been trying to carry on the work that was started."

Some people gasped and whispered as Sky made her way to the microphone. Pharaoh continued,

"She recently came under fire, but I would like to welcome her today as a daughter of Ms. Jessie."

Pharaoh hugged Sky and the sanctuary clapped. Marlon and Paris were surprised. Paris did not know Pharaoh knew Sky. Marlon did not know Miss. Jessie helped Sky.

Sky began,

"Miss Jessie inspired me to start the Maker's House. Her house was the only place I felt safe once I entered the foster care system. When Preston Johnson died at the Maker's House facility I thought to myself. This would have never happened at Miss. Jessie's House. She was a protector, a mother, and she saved so many of us. She called me when everything first started and reassured me that there would be Justice. Her message was always. You are worthy of love no matter who you are and what you are. If anyone ever discards you retrieve yourself because you are your best thing. Her second message, it's never too late to change. Take up your shield of faith share your testimony and help somebody and recognize that there is a God.

Miss Jessie taught me that it is ok, to tell the truth, and be yourself. I did not understand it as a child, but I understand now. I myself am a sinner. We all are sinners and no one is perfect. I asked the Lord for forgiveness. I have also asked some of those I have wronged to forgive me and I have a long line of people to ask. The Lord is only asking us to come with a heart that wants to do the right thing. Do not be ashamed and this is what Ma Jessie reinforced."

Pharaoh stood beside Sky and when her words started to crackle he stepped back up to the mic and picked up where Sky left off.

"She helped many of us, but not many of you know Miss Jessie. I was given the gift and the honor of spending her last days with her. She wanted me to tell all of you who she really was.  She was forced to grow up too fast when her parents died and many took advantage of her. They took advantage of her so much that at the age of twelve she was riding a bike and had her first miscarriage simply by trying to enjoy being a child. She didn't even know what being pregnant was. She was forced to sell her body full time by the time she was fifteen.   She went on to become a drug addict to kill the pain of being raped and used. She said God spoke to her and that is when she left her pimp in Lousiana and fled to Boston. She got here, got clean, and started working.  She has many names of endearment that is why whatever name you called her Ma Jessie, Miss Jessie, Grandma Jessie, or Auntie Jessie had so much love in her heart. She never judged others. She bought a house and turned it into love. If you have ever looked in her eyes then you saw God in her. The God that holds no judgment and the God that loves you. Before she was a member of Binka she was a Christian.  Even though she was a member of Binka she never stopped being a Christian. I remember the song she used to sing when I was a child. It was called repent. It's not a pretty song but it's real.He started to sing,

"There is an old song for the old and young.

If you are weary all you have to do is call the one.

Who died for you, and died for me, confess and he will make you clean.

Take me home, take me home, take me home, take me home."

The choir stood and almost everyone in the sanctuary joined in.

After the song Sky announced. "We are going to take communion. If you all would please reach in front of you there you will find the provisions to do so. The word of God says that we should examine ourselves before we take communion. Think of everyone you need to forgive and release

Dr. Malcam realized they were all taking communion at the same time. The congregation in red tried to depart the sanctuary. The massive crowd made it almost impossible for them to move quickly. They tried to pass through a crowd with over six hundred people in attendance. It was then he realized Sky was going to summon the holy spirit. "God's word says in Matthew 26:26-30 'While they were eating, Jesus took bread, and when he had given thanks, he broke it and gave it to his disciples, saying, "Take and eat; this is my body." Then he took a cup, and when he had given thanks, he gave it to them, saying, "Drink from it, all of you. This is my blood of the covenant, which is poured out for many for the forgiveness of sins." The two elders, Solace, and the congregation all drank and then they all ate. Sky then said,

"Scripture also tells us in 1 John 4:4 'Ye are of God, little children, and have overcome them: because greater is he that is in you, than he that is in the world." Sky moved back away from the microphone as Pharaoh approached it again. She moved closer to Dr. Abishai, stood next to him, and dropped salt around her feet. He looked down at the salt she was releasing and moved away from her towards the edge of the stage.

Dr. Malcam walked down from the pulpit as the congregation started to worship louder.  The sound of worship agitated the Binka congregation as they aggressively approached the exit to leave. The worship was invoking the presence of the Holy Spirit. People started crying and praying.  Sky knelt and then lay her belly on the altar and let the words flow.

She cried out,

" lem la ke, tekem betem nom na sem boon. Tekka lat foon bel lan sek tekem."  The petition prayer commenced and was released from her mouth, requesting the Holy Spirit to break the yoke. Solace, Love, and Makeda surrounded her like a shield. The funeral of Miss Jessie turned into worship to the Lord. People were crying out for mercy and more and more people flooded the altar asking the Lord for forgiveness. The Binka congregation and Dr. Malcam finally arrived at the church entrance. As they exited it looked like it had finished raining as the ground was wet. Dr. Malcam inhaled and smelled flowers and earth and he was filled with concern.  In the distance on the horizon, he was able to see a rainbow and he knew the Angel of death had descended into the earth realm. Abishai was in a furious rush to leave. As he walked down the church steps with his congregation Dr. Malcam felt the presence of the Holy Spirit and the demon baby gnats departed from him.  Above his head, he saw over a thousand angels assembled in armor. He tried to look up again, but his eyes were blinded by light and diamonds. Dr. Malcam could feel other spirits and demons departing from the other members of his congregation.   Just then, He was anchored in place and could not move. Several of his members tried to help him move but they could not move him.  The two captive spirits stopped walking and requested that the angel of death hear their testimony and deliver their moans and grief to the Holy Spirit. The captive spirits moaned to the angel of death begging for rest and mercy. that they were being unfairly held as they did not agree to the deal Tuma made all those years ago. They asked the Holy Spirit for peace and relief. The Holy spirit severed the yoke and bond between Dakarai, Tuma, Marlon, Sky, Paris, and Pharaoh. All of the bonds were broken and they were untethered.  The angel of death granted Dakarai and Bala entry into rest in the realm of the dead.   Once the captive spirits departed from Dr. Malcam he was able to move again.

The people attending the funeral were starting to flow out of the church in order to follow to the cemetery.  At the cemetery, few words were spoken. Pharaoh and Sky watched Marlon and Paris hold each other and their wounded hearts broke as Miss Jessie was lowered into the ground.  Makeda held Sky's hand on the right and Solace held her other hand on the left. Love stood next to Pharoah. Everything gets buried today. Sky declared.

Abishai was cold on his way home.  He started to shiver. He went to the lab in his basement immediately and pulled vials to appease Tuma's spirit.  He felt multiple spirits come into the room one by one, which made him shake not only from the cold but nervousness.  Then flies began to gather. Covering his vials of blood.

"I am gathering," Abishai reassured. The demon Baby Gnats laughed and proclaimed.

"Those vials cannot feed all of us if we are hungry."
Dr. Abishai clutched his chest in pain as the spirit of Tuma
from the past approached him.  You promised that I would
have his love in the last life and I did not and you promised
I would have his love in this life.

The angry spirit Tuma grew more infuriated. The more the
spirit recalled her unrequited love and how she was
robbed by the Shifter who is now Doctor Abishai Malcam.
The unfairness of it all enraged her. Her life on earth had
been written by circumstance. Born into royalty, unable to
love who she wanted, then deceived and cheated by the
Shifter. She was no longer on the earth plane. The demon
Baby Gnats allowed The Shifter to hide on the earth realm
as long as he was fed blood.

The angry spirit Tuma called more spirits that were
enraged that he was still on the earth realm. The amount
of blood he was able to spill to achieve his existence was
not enough today. The lies and the humans that sold their
souls to him. He had grown fat and sloppy from all of his
deals and deeds. Unable to fulfill the debt he owed, They
began to consume him.  Dr. Malcam could feel them
draining him. He departed his basement and ascended the
steps slowly. His legs were heavy and stiff. His eye twitched
and suddenly he was insatiably thirsty.  He gasped for air
as he finally reached the top of the steps. He saw the
bathroom at the end of the hallway and his body was
growing heavier and heavier with each step.

When he finally reached the bathroom he filled the
tub with water. His tub was deep and it was taking longer
than he wanted to fill up.  The cold, chest pains, heaviness,
shaking, and cramping in his fingers was nothing compared

to the squeals he started to hear.  Dr. Malcam slowly climbed into the tub and lay back in the hot water.  The pain and squeals stopped immediately. He thought to himself  *YES, YES, YES,YES, YES!!!!* His cramped fingers loosened. His body gained warmth again. He lifted his nose and mouth to the surface of the water to breathe and then went back under the water.  Abishai repeated this ritual several times until he gathered the courage to submerge himself and breathe the water in deeply. He fell into the equivalent of the transition of being awake and sleep and then finally he slept under water. When he woke up he jerked up and gasped for air. Water splashed all over the floor. He wasn't sure if he achieved death this time.  The bathroom was quiet. No squeals or the smell of sulfur and his body was not attacking him. He lay back into the water and smiled. *I did it again*. He thought to himself.

He slowly stood and reached for a towel.  He dried his face, stomach, and arms and then proceeded to put one foot out of the tub. Just then, the angry spirit Tuma startled him and he slipped on the water beneath his foot and hit his head on the tub with great force. Warm blood slowly gushed from his head down his neck to his back and eventually to the floor. He was dizzy and the blood kept coming and the spirits and the previous pains returned. The spirits positioned themselves to consume his blood. His chest tightened and he blinked slowly as memories flashed. The blood extraction was excruciatingly painful. Just then, when he was almost drained. He smelled roses and saw the beautiful diamond wings.  The angel of death was crying for him. He felt peace.

"Is it my time?" Abishai asked the angel.

"It's been your time." The angel replied.

"Where are you taking me? He asked her.

"I am taking you to Father God, and he will decide where you're going." She replied.

Dr. Abishai Malcam felt comfort in her response and departed the earth realm with her.

## 22

## Obituary of The Dishonorable

The Honorable Dr. Abishai Malcam was born March 10, 1935 in Edgefield South Carolina to Louis and Eakkon Flakes. As the child of sharecroppers, not much is known about his early life or childhood. He left the south and traveled to Boston for college in 1953. He earned his Bachelor of Arts and went on to medical school.  As one of the first to integrate many of the colleges and universities, the road to success was filled with many obstacles. Dr. Malcam's intelligence was unmatched and he quickly rose through the ranks. He became one of the first Black Medical Doctors and Psychiatrists to acquire his own medical facility and treatment centers.

He is one of the most respected and premier voices in the African American male and female community. His research focused on the after-effects of slavery, reconstruction, sharecropping, segregation, and the post-traumatic stress of survivors of these horrible events and their offspring.  He is praised for his work with children and his track record for curing many mental health issues that are related to and plagued the black community. He is hailed for single handedly developing psychotropic drugs designed, tested, and proven to work on people of African descent. He designed the method for including people of color in medical trials and testing. His ground-breaking research and cure for HIV and AIDS have propelled the medical community forward. His life work was extensive as he is the author of five books entitled *The Sacred things belong to Us, Generational Curses, Ambrosia, Inner Vows, Sanctuary Chambers, and Hidden in the Blood.*

He is the owner of various health centers and funeral homes in Dorchester and Roxbury. His philanthropic generosity toward prison reform is unmatched. He secured finances and started his program for reform that included intense therapy with a low recidivism rate.

Dr. Malcam had many academic achievements but he considered his creation of the religion of Binka to be his greatest accomplishment. The focus of Binka was establishing equality through knowledge and empowering his congregation to own their own destiny.  Dr. Malcam did not have children but he is survived by his congregation whom he considered to be family.  A pillar in the community and great humanitarian to the world we are saddened to say goodbye to a great man.  He passed away on December 12, 2019, of natural causes.

After Sky finished reading his obituary, she sat the phone on her desk and looked outside.  She could not believe this really happened in her life.  She folded her arms and rubbed her hand up and down her arm.  She knew he passed shortly after Miss Jessie, but this was the first time she read his actual obituary.  She straightened the folders on her desk and reviewed the reunification plan for two of the children from the Maker's House. She was pleased that they would be going back home. She looked at her watch and gathered her things. The visions and interruptions in the middle of the day stopped.  She got her bag and told Sharon ``I'll see you tonight." She walked through the cobblestone streets of Boston towards the train. She had to bob and weave through the people the closer she got to the green line.  Spring was in the air and her jacket was too heavy.  She walked down Park Street and entered the musty, hot crowded red line station. She waited on the antiquated platform annoyed like everyone else by the terrible service. She kept herself busy by checking her text with an occasional bump or two from other riders. Suddenly Dejavu hit her. She had been here before. Her body felt warm and the hairs on her arms lifted. She stopped and glanced across the platform. She would recognize that shape anywhere. Marlon looked back at her. She looked at him and at that moment, a pair of lips kissed his cheek from the woman who had to stand on her tippy toes to reach him.  The woman definitely was not Paris. As he looked at Sky The music from the subway performer stopped and the chattering muted. It seemed as if everyone else disappeared and it was just them. Sky broke away from their glance, turned around, and proceeded to walk in the opposite direction down to the end of the platform as if she had just seen a ghost.  She was not compelled to say hello. Her face remained stoic, her body did not betray her, and she did not yearn for his conversation or touch.  She remembered the lessons from the realms. She was relieved that the train finally arrived while she was walking toward the end of the platform and she was able to get on the last train car. She sat down in a corner seat on the train and proceeded to read Dr. Malcam's obituary again.  The ride to Ashmont was filled with flashes of the last six months. If she did not live this experience, she would not believe it herself.  When she arrived at Ashmont she walked upstairs and put on her coat as not to attract the attention of the men.

Solace blew her horn and Sky got in the car.

"What's up with you? You look like you saw a ghost." Solace jokes. They both laughed.

"I did," Sky replied.  "I saw Marlon."  Solace put her head down and looked at her with the glasses she was wearing.

"What happened?" Solace asked.

"Nothing." Sky replied with raised eyebrows.

"Did you say anything?" Solace impatiently inquired and gestured her hands to say move the story along.

Sky explained, "Not a word and neither did he. I saw him, he saw me, we made eye contact and then some woman kissed him."

"SOME WOMAN?" Solace belted out theatrically as she pulled the car over. "Not his woman, Paris?."Solace asked to clarify.

"Yeah, some other woman but not Paris." Sky confirmed.

Solace looked at her friend for signs of sadness or regret but she saw none.

Sky interrupted Solaces' stare, "I walked the other way and I felt nothing."

"That's awesome," Solace responded.  "The Lord is still working on me. I would have gave him these hands if it were me." She assured Sky as she sucked her teeth.

"Was that the first time you felt nothing?" Solace asked.

"Yes, it was the first time. I couldn't believe it. I was so wounded I didn't think I could get over it, but today I was over it all." Sky said with pride.

Solace confirmed, "Well, you did the work. I was there when you sweat him off your spirit." Solace reached over to hug Sky and Sky hugged her back.

"Thanks for sending me the obituary." Sky said with relief in her voice.

"What did you think?" Solace asked.

"I have mixed feelings" Sky confessed

Mixed feelings, How? Solace inquired.

"I can't believe he passed." Solace said with a tone of surprise in her voice.

"Girl bye! That man was condemned by what he approved. That's what the Bible says." Solace confirmed.

Sky began to count the miracles on her fingers as she recalled,

"Hold up, at the same time it's confirmation. I never thought I would see my mother again, I can't believe the Maker's House was exonerated and I never thought I could live without Marlon. I think how many more people there are out there with these things happening to them and they are going through what I just went through, but they can't see the spiritual things. They don't have the people to help them."

Solace gently reminded Sky, "Yeah, but they have God and he sends the angels and the holy spirit is on the earth. Also, people and prophets are called to help. Evil will not go unchecked.

They finally pulled up to the ugly store in the field on Norfolk Street, surrounded by gentrification. When they entered there were people waiting in the store on the brown leather couch as usual.  They greeted them as they walked by.  Makeda and Love were waiting downstairs.

"Ya'll are late!" Love barked. Sky hugged Makeda and Love hugged Solace.  Makeda began speaking,

"The woman we are seeing tonight says that she kept waking up outside of nursing homes with empty vials. She is organizing a biotechnology conference and becomes dazed and confused at work. She insists that these vials she makes contain a disease that is going to shut down the whole world. She says she does not remember how she got to these places and why she was there. Hopefully, we can help her. Love started to hold hands with Makeda, Solace, and Sky.

"Before we welcome her in, we have to prepare. LET'S PRAY! Guard your gates, everybody." Love commanded.

## Other books:

1.  _____Everything is True By Teisha Brown
    (My former last name) Also known as
    Teisha Christie

www.ingramcontent.com/pod-product-compliance
Lightning Source LLC
Chambersburg PA
CBHW020548020726
47494CB00006B/1977